I0599398

MURDER IN THE NUDIST CLUB

BOOKS IN THE ARGOSY LIBRARY:

MURDER IN THE NUDIST CLUB

FRED MacISAAC

ILLUSTRATED BY
JOSEPH A. FARREN

COVER BY
LEJAREN HILLER

POPULAR PUBLICATIONS · 2024

© 2024 Popular Publications, an imprint of Steeger Properties, LLC

First Edition—2024

PUBLISHING HISTORY

"Murder in the Nudist Club" originally appeared in the August 18, 25, September 1, 8, 15, 1934 issues of *Detective Fiction Weekly* magazine (Vol. 87, Nos. 1–5). Copyright © 1934 by The Frank A. Munsey Company. Copyright renewed © 1961 and assigned to Steeger Properties, LLC. All rights reserved.

ALL RIGHTS RESERVED

No part of this book may be reproduced or utilized in any form or by any means without permission in writing from the publisher.

Visit argosymagazine.com for more books like this.

TABLE OF CONTENTS

MURDER IN THE NUDIST CLUB

*The Lovely Mona Thompson Lay
Dead, and Somewhere in that Garden
of Eden Lurked a Naked Murderer*

1

"WHAT? NO NUDISTS?"

MR. WILLIAM DUFFY, managing editor of the San Diego *Sphere,* emitted a grunt indicating eager expectancy as Dick Hoban, his star camera man approached bearing a huge sheet of cardboard, which he proudly placed upon the boss's desk. On the cardboard lay a dozen wet photographic prints at which Duffy stared and emitted a second grunt, this time signifying bitter disappointment.

"Swell, eh?" inquired the camera man.

"Rotten. I charter a plane. I borrow a military camera. And what do you get? Landscapes, by heaven!"

"Aw, Bill, I got pictures of the whole joint. The pond, the grove, the clubhouse—"

"Where are the beautiful young naked women?"

"Well, boss, everybody run under the trees when they saw me coming."

"I send him after nudists at play," mourned Mr. Duffy, "and he brings me samples of still life. Faugh, Mr. Hoban! Faugh, I say! Phooey!"

"They're the first pictures of the interior of the Santa Rosalita Nudist Club," protested the camera man.

"Go away before I sock you on the nose. Take these architect's blue prints with you."

When the camera man had departed, Bill leaned back,

*He climbed on a packing
box and peered out*

crossed his legs and scowled at the smoke laden atmosphere.

A few more fiascos like this and there would be a new face at the desk of the managing editor. He had had plenty trouble persuading the publisher to spend seventy dollars and he had nothing to show for it.

Mr. Duffy, referred to by his staff as "Wild William," had been a successful New York reporter when he met a girl from San Diego who was visiting in the East. Being a young man of masterful tendencies, he had rushed this young woman until she consented to become his bride and accepted, with blissful transports, a platinum ring containing a diamond about the size of the head of a pin.

The idea was that she would return to her home. When he had saved up some money, he was to proceed to San Diego and marry the girl. At the train he presented her with a half dozen orchids and twelve pounds of candy.

When months had passed and she had ignored letters

*Suddenly one of the bare
young maidens screamed*

and telegrams he threw up his job and journeyed to San
Diego to find out what was the matter.

The day Bill Duffy arrived in San Diego, Iris—her name
was Iris Dalton—was being married in a cathedral at high
noon to a lieutenant-commander in the Navy. The happy
pair moved away from the altar under an arch of swords.
Mr. Duffy went out and got drunk.

By and by he landed a reporter's job on the morning
Sphere at a salary an office boy in New York would have
scorned. As he now hated women and liquor was legal,
he rose rapidly to be managing editor. One of the reasons
he had risen so speedily to high command was that the
publisher of the *Sphere* fired managing editors for slight
reason. Spending seventy dollars fruitlessly was not a slight
reason. Bill was worried.

He gave routine dictation to his stenographer, a young woman chosen as much for her plainness as her efficiency, and was oblivious to the approach of a stranger until he was hailed.

"How are you, Bill?" asked the stranger.

He was a big man, brawny, with hairy hands. His rough features were well assembled, considering their type, and he owned a pair of cold, hard, blue eyes and a smile which had a lot to recommend it. He looked to be about thirty-five and he might have been mistaken for a stevedore had it not been for the eyes and a broad, high forehead.

"HELLO, BRADY," SAID Bill Duffy. "Long way from home, eh?"

Mr. Brady seated himself, pulled out two cigars, offered one to the editor.

"Didn't expect to find you away out here. I came in to ask permission to use your morgue."

"And why not? Miss Wayne, let me introduce to you Mr. Jack Brady, head of the Brady Detective Agency of New York, formerly the ace of the Secret Service and, aside from that, a good egg."

The secretary bobbed her head.

"Staying at the U.S. Grant Hotel?"

"Nope. I'm a guest of Thomas P. Thompson at Santa Rosalita."

Mr. Duffy's black eyes narrowed. "Yeah? What's up over there?"

"Oh, nothing."

"Friend of yours?"

"In a way."

"Jack, if there's a story, for God's sake spill it. I'm going to walk the plank if I don't turn up a sensation pretty soon."

"Nothing to say. I'm in rather a hurry. Can I use your morgue?"

"Sure. Miss Wayne, take this oyster to the morgue. He ought to be on a slab in a real one."

"When I can spill something, Bill, you get it exclusive," said Brady as he rose.

"And I've heard that before," remarked the managing editor bitterly.

When his secretary had returned he had instructions for her. "Wait ten minutes, slip into the morgue, and find out what obituary envelopes Brady asked for. Don't let him get wise. Maybe I can put two and two together as well as that big stiff."

He waited impatiently until she had performed her mission and placed before him a slip of paper on which were written the following names: Mr. Thomas P. Thompson. Mrs. Thomas P. Thompson (Mona Morgan), Owen Overman, Lida Sterling.

"Something doing over there, something doing," muttered the newspaper man. "Brady's there professionally. What is it? Murder? Robbery? Miss Wayne—" aloud—"I'm going to be taken sick in a little while. I may be confined to my bed for a few days. Tell Clark to carry on. Rum-tittle-tittle, rum-tittle-to."

"I beg your pardon, Mr. Duffy."

"I'm feverish—that's a symptom."

The entrance of the detective caused Mr. Duffy to become his usual businesslike self.

"Come out with me and have a cup of coffee," suggested Mr. Brady.

"And why not?" inquired Bill, who reached for his hat. Tell Clark, Miss Wayne."

"Yes, sir." Miss Wayne gazed after him mournfully. While she liked Mr. Duffy very much, she had long been convinced he was so crazy that sooner or later they would back up an ambulance in front of the *Sphere* office and take him where he belonged.

"I've great news for you, Jack," declared Duffy as they seated themselves in a lunch-room. "I'm going back to Santa Rosalita with you tonight. I'm going to lose my job, old man, unless I crash the Nudist Club."

"Nudist Club?"

"Thompson's, on Rosalita. I sent a camera man in a plane over today and he got nothing. I'm on a spot."

"But nudist clubs are no novelty," said Brady. "All you have to do is pay a fee, take off your clothes and walk in."

"This one is different. Exclusive. High jinks go on there. Famous people in wild orgies—"

"Rubbish. What do you know about Thompson?"

"King Tom? The big utilities magnate. He bought the island ten years ago when it was a desert. He has made it bloom. Made it one of the most popular resorts on the coast. It's a gold mine."

"I mean personally."

"Oh. He's an old so and so. Won't give newspaper men a break."

"I only spent a few hours there. He is sole owner of the island and rules it with a high hand, I gathered."

"Sure. A newspaper man is watched and put on the first

steamer if he leaves the public zone and tries to get near the club. How about taking me back with you?"

"Nothing doing. I'm working for Thompson—"

"So. What's happened? Murder? Robbery?"

"My boy, I have nothing to give out. Thompson, it appears, owns his own police force and the County officers leave him entirely alone, eh?"

"For heaven's sake, Brady."

"I'll tell you this much, confidentially."

"I don't want confidential information. I want something I can print."

"I'm sorry. Have you ever heard rumors of smuggling from Santa Rosalita?"

"There's smuggling everywhere. Listen. Is Thompson dead?"

"No."

"Then who is?"

"I have told you that I can tell you nothing for publication."

"You're there because a crime has been committed. King Tom is keeping it dark. That's being accessory after the fact. I'm going to get the district attorney of Resalvo County—"

"Suppose you do that," said Brady. "Old man, I'm going to send some telegrams and am asking the replies to be sent care of you at the *Sphere*. Will you keep them for me?"

"O.K.," said Duffy sullenly.

Brady rose. "I'm leaving on Thompson's speed cruiser immediately. Bill, there is a tremendous story over there. I'll give you the first information possible."

"O.K., cop."

2

MR. DUFFY LOSES HIS PANTS

THE MORNING EXCURSION steamer *Naida,* carrying one hundred fifty passengers and William Duffy, was approaching the breakwater of Santa Rosalita. Bill was at the bow, gazing eagerly forward. He was not wearing green whiskers. He had never visited the big island located fifty miles out to sea from San Diego; he didn't anticipate that any of the island officials would recognize him as a newspaper man.

Hanging by a strap from his shoulders was a leather case which presumably held binoculars and which marked him as a tourist. He was wearing golf knickers and a cap. His appearance had caused several young girls aboard the steamer to giggle but Bill wanted to appear harmless and he was indifferent to female laughter.

Inside the binocular case, as it happened, was a fine German camera. Bill did not propose to leave Santa Rosalita without getting inside the Nudist Club.

He could see the Club from the deck of the ship, being familiar with its appearance from the "landscapes" captured by his camera man.

Santa Rosalita was an island which had been compared to Capri because its cliffs rise abruptly from the ocean. It is about ten miles wide and twenty miles long, and its highest peak is over fifteen hundred feet. King Tom's great white house was plainly visible upon a crag eight hundred feet high, overlooking the town.

The town itself had been built on the shore, at the mouth of a canyon which penetrated some distance into the interior, climbing swiftly.

About a mile from the beach and the village, upon a sort of plateau, stood the building and grounds of the Nudist Club at which Bill gazed eagerly. A high stucco wall extended for several hundred yards; above it could be seen a white flat-roofed building with red tile trimmings, and the tops of a grove of trees. From the pictures Bill knew that the grounds of the Club were a dozen acres in extent; that there was a large swimming pool, practically a lake; thick soft turf for naked tootsies; grateful shade when the island sun was blistering; and a membership which was most exclusive.

Duffy's chief interest in this particular Nudist Club was its membership, which included famous people: film stars, artists who had built cottages on the island. Thompson's guests, who were automatically club members, included many socially prominent people. Bill thought it would be nice if he could get pictures of such people in their birthday suits. Since they were willing to parade about like that at the Club, they ought not to resent being pictured nude on the front page of the *Sphere*. Anyway, they couldn't sue the paper for libel. The camera does not lie.

The effect of such photographs upon the future of the subjects didn't interest him. He was a newspaper nut who didn't worry about things like that.

There was something queer about the village, he thought. Few people were visible. A red motor boat came out from behind the breakwater as the steamer entered the opening and a man in her bow began to wigwag. There was a jangle of bells from the bridge and the engines stopped, while the ship drifted into the harbor on momentum. The motor boat came alongside and a uniformed police officer came up the ladder, to be met at the rail by the ship's captain. Bill Duffy edged close.

"What's the trouble?" he heard the captain demand.

"Quarantine," replied the officer. "Smallpox. Three cases at the hospital. You can't land passengers. Orders are for you to return to the mainland."

"What shall I say to my passengers?"

"Whatever you like. Nobody can enter or leave the island until the quarantine is lifted."

BILL DUFFY WAITED to hear no more. He moved away, elbowing through the crowd, went swiftly down to the lower deck. At the stern of the ship, the rail wasn't more than six feet above the water. Duffy kicked off his shoes, tied the shoestrings together and hung his brogans around his neck; then after making sure that he was unobserved, he went over the stern rail and dropped with a plop into the sea.

Bill was aware that if the propeller started to turn over at that moment he would be chopped into mincemeat, but a newspaper man has to take a chance.

He sank into the blue depths, struck out fiercely, came to the surface twenty feet from the ship. If he was observed, he might be dragged on board. There was a low black motor boat moored just inside the breakwater a hundred feet away. It appeared to be untenanted and he struck out for it.

Fortunately for his purpose, which was to get ashore on Rosalita in defiance of smallpox, cholera or anything else, all eyes on the ship were turned toward shore. He reached the low waist of the motor boat, pulled himself on board and flung himself flat on the deck.

After that he pulled off his clothes, spread them out to dry, went into the little cabin and stretched himself on a leather bunk.

In his opinion the quarantine was phony. Thompson could do anything on Santa Rosalita. He had closed the port for the same reason he had sent for the detective. Smallpox would keep the County officers away. Bill knew the kind of officers they had in the rural County of Resalvo, which had jurisdiction over the island.

Presently he heard a slight bump on deck. He stuck his head up through the hatchway and pulled it in again like a turtle.

There was a dripping Venus on deck; a tall, slender, shapely girl in a wisp of a yellow bathing suit which blended so perfectly with her golden tan that she might just as well not have worn it. She had in her hands Bill Duffy's pants and she was just about to stick her wet hand in his pocket.

"Hey, drop those pants," said Mr. Duffy roughly. Instead of obeying she stepped to the hatch and peeked down. Bill cowered, protecting himself from curious female eyes as best he could.

"A nudist," remarked the girl. "How shocking."

"Have a heart, will you?" he whined. "Throw me them pants."

"Open that locker behind the right hand bunk. You'll find overalls. After that come up and give an account of yourself," she said sternly.

Covered with blue denim, Bill climbed on deck. She was sitting on his coat and had pulled his golf trousers over her naked thighs.

"This is my boat," she said. "What's the idea?"

"I was on the excursion steamer, and when I heard about the quarantine I went overboard. You see I planned on a vacation here and I—"

"What's your name?"

"Bill Duffy. What's yours?"

"Never mind," she said cheerfully. "You look sort of cute in those overalls."

"You looked better before you put on my pants," he replied. This young woman had much yellow hair and a small round pert face and oversized blue eyes and a fascinating grin. Apparently she rather liked the idea of finding a young, fairly good looking man on her boat.

"I laid them out to dry and you're getting them wet," he added grumpily.

"Aren't you afraid of smallpox?"

"No. I think the quarantine's phony."

"Then you know about the murder at the Nudist Club!" she exclaimed excitedly.

"Sure." Bill was ten times as much excited. A murder. And at the Nudist Club.

"How do you know about it?" he asked cautiously.

"Why, I was there when they found poor Mona."

"Mona Thompson, Thompson's wife? Was she murdered?"

"Then you didn't know anything about it at all?" she gasped.

"Sure. I'm a friend of John Brady, the detective. I'm his assistant."

She clasped her hands. "How exciting! It's all right if you knew about it. We promised Mr. Thompson we would say nothing until the murderer was caught."

Bill sat right down beside her.

"You mean you were there—"

"I was in the Club—it was late—I'd fallen asleep. Most everybody was gone when they found her."

"You mean—you're a nudist?" he exclaimed.

She turned and opened eyes as big as pansies and as gorgeous.

"Nudism is nothing," she stated blandly.

"Yeah, never mind. About Mrs. Thompson. What time did they find her? How was she killed?"

She eyed him sharply. "I don't think you know anything about it. Do you know what I think? You're a reporter."

"Right, lady, and a good one. Come on now. Somebody shot Mrs. Thompson or stabbed her. Give me the facts. Jumping mackerel, what a story!"

THE YOUNG WOMAN leaped to her feet. Bill leaped to his feet also and faced her eagerly. She laid her right palm gently on his chest, pushed suddenly and with amazing force. Mr. Duffy staggered back and overboard. When he came up, she was casting off the mooring line. He succeeded in getting his hands on the side of the speed boat. She started the engine. Bill was half over the side when she swooped upon him and thrust him back into the water. The craft was moving.

"My pants," he wailed. The girl pulled them off and with a laugh tossed them into the water, then picking up his various articles of clothing threw them after the trousers. Last came the camera.

Disregarding the garments, Duffy dove for the leather case and retrieved it, after which he captured golf pants and coat and shirt, which were sinking slowly. By this time the young woman had taken the wheel and was driving her speed boat rapidly across the little harbor.

Bill was almost sobbing.

"I'll get even with her," he kept repeating. "The blond devil, I'll make her wish she hadn't been born."

Ten minutes later, arrayed in wet clothes and utterly regardless of his appearance, he rushed into a telephone pay station, dropped a coin in the phone and cried excitedly to the operator, "Give me San Diego, the *Sphere* office."

"I'm sorry," central said, "something has happened to the cable to the mainland. All lines are temporarily cut off."

William Duffy emerged dolefully from the phone booth. A great story. A tremendous story. The murder of the wife of the owner of Rosalita Island at the Nudist Club—and he couldn't get the story away.

3

BRADY'S STORY

AWARE THAT HE was a suspicious looking object in his dripping garments and bare feet, Duffy walked slowly along the boulevard which ran around the crescent of the beach.

Well, if he couldn't get the story away, neither could anybody else. The cable had been cut, of course. The radio station belonged to Thompson. Newspapermen were unpopular at all times with King Tom; with a murder being covered up, the local cops would thrust a reporter in the jug.

He turned into a bathing pavilion, rented a bathing suit, and hung up his clothes in a locker. In an hour or so they would be dry. He crossed the paved street—the asphalt was very hot on the soles of his feet, ran across the beach and went into the water. There were scores of bathers and hundreds more lying on the beach in skimpy bathing costumes, letting their pores drink in the bright sunlight.

He went up on the beach and got into conversation with several people. These were very much excited about the quarantine, but took it for granted there was good reason for it. They were half frightened because of the presence on the island of smallpox, and half delighted because the owner of the island had announced that tourists held on

Santa Rosalita by the quarantine would have free meals and lodgings until it was lifted.

Obviously, none of them knew that the wife of Thomas P. Thompson had been murdered.

When an hour had passed Duffy returned to the bath house, dressed himself and sauntered forth, his supposed binoculars bumping against his hip.

The bathing pavilion was opposite the pier head. At the right side of the pier entrance was a small building over the door of which was the sign "U.S. Customs." And as Duffy was crossing the street, the door opened and Detective Jack Brady came forth. Bill hesitated. Brady might have him locked up and deported, since he was in the employ of Thompson. Brady espied him—he saw everything apparently—looked surprised, and beckoned.

"So you got ashore," he said.

"You going to turn me in?" asked Duffy sullenly.

"I don't think so. How did you get here?"

"Came on the morning steamer."

"But she was turned back."

"I slipped overboard. What's doing, Jack?"

"Why, nothing."

Bill grinned.

"Who killed Mrs. Thompson?" he asked softly.

The detective stared at him and then his lips twitched.

"How in hell did you learn that?" he demanded. "Have you notified your paper?"

"Don't you know the cable has been cut?"

"I did not."

"I thought maybe you suggested it, along with this comical quarantine."

"I didn't suggest that, either," said Brady. "Let's take a walk out to the end of the pier. There is a peculiar situation here. Maybe we can help each other."

"I'm hearing nothing in confidence, remember."

Brady laughed. "With the cable cut, a quarantine on and what not, you'll have to respect my confidence."

They walked about a hundred yards along the pier and seated themselves on a bench. The harbor of Santa Rosalita had been an indentation in the rocky coastline, across which Thompson at great expense had thrust a breakwater. While small, it provided safe anchorage for a host of small craft, yachts, speed boats and fishing boats; and there was a fifteen foot channel which permitted excursion steamers to tie up at the pier, from where they sat they had a marvelous view of the island. Its hills rose abruptly, great brown rock piles upon which were suspended villas of pink and white and blue and green, Spanish or Italian in style. All habitations on the island had been built and were owned by Thompson, who leased them at high rentals to persons whom he considered desirable neighbors.

The village faced the beach, a typical resort, with shops and amusement places lining the landward side of the boulevard. Its side streets climbed the hills for a very short distance. One of them wound its way up the canyon and ended at the Nudist Club.

BRADY STUDIED DUFFY covertly. Between detectives and newspapermen there is a mutual liking mingled with distrust. In a sense they are competitors and, when allied, it is with mental reservations.

Brady knew Bill Duffy to be an especially shrewd and alert young man. His employer was determined upon secrecy. Under ordinary circumstances he would have had no truck with Bill Duffy but the circumstances were not ordinary.

"Bill," he said, "I was in Los Angeles yesterday morning on business. I was waked up by a radio from Thompson, telling me there was a plane waiting to bring me here and I could name my own fee. I arrived shortly before noon. I met Thompson at his house.

"He told me that his wife had been strangled to death during the night and do you know what he did? He sent the butler up with me to view the body."

"Cool customer. Did he seem badly cut up?"

"He was positively surly. It looked as if he was furious because somebody belonging to him had been killed but he didn't act like a man stricken with grief."

"I've heard he was a brute."

"He said he wanted the murderer punished, even if it was one of his own sons. He hadn't notified the County authorities, claiming that the cable to the mainland had broken off."

"But radioed you, you say."

"Yes. He said he didn't want fools muddling up the case. He was waiting to radio when I had captured the murderer. Well, I went up to Mrs. Thompson's room. You never saw such a place, Bill. The room is thirty feet square, with great windows which open on a balcony. There is a bathroom with a Roman pool. Here's a funny thing—the walls are padded, absolutely sound-proof. So are all the rooms in the house. Well, lying on a great silver bed, under a silver satin sheet was a woman, hardly more than a girl, with platinum hair. Beautiful, Bill. I took a look at her and I recognized her. She used to be an artist's model in New York and then went on the stage. Name of Mona Morgan. She was this fellow's fourth wife."

"We've a lot of pictures of her. The wedding made a big stir a couple of years ago."

"She had been strangled. Rigor mortis had set in. The most pitiful part of it is that she was several months pregnant."

"What a story!"

"I had insisted that the local chief of police be sent for. He is a stupid little man who knows nothing. We searched the place and didn't find a clue."

"No finger marks on the neck?"

"She was strangled with a towel or beneath a pillow."

Duffy nodded. "Go on."

"Well, aside from Thompson and Mona, four people spent the night in the house. His son and wife, a young woman named Lida Sterling, and a novelist named Owen Overman, who is doing Thompson's biography. They were all there. I questioned each one. The Sterling woman is supposed to be Thompson's friend. There was bad blood between her and Mrs. Thompson."

"Think one of them did it?"

"I don't know. It's possible that the crime was committed by an outsider. While the grounds are guarded, it wouldn't be hard for a murderer to come over the roof of the porch and enter through the chamber window."

"Interesting," said Duffy with an enigmatic smile.

"Well, Thompson, late yesterday afternoon, demanded the name of the murderer. When I told him I hadn't a clue as yet he bawled me out, told me he had no use for my services and suggested that I leave the island. I refused. I said I never dropped a case and didn't give a damn about my fee. I told him he must radio the County officers immediately and that the thing couldn't be hushed up as apparently he wished it.

"He changed his tune and apologized, told me to go ahead. He promised to notify the County officers. I presume that's why he clapped on this quarantine. Catch the district attorney and sheriff coming in here to be held until the quarantine is lifted. Of course, he claims that there is smallpox."

"That all?" asked Duffy.

"I slipped out of the house last night," said Brady, "forced the chief of police to let me take Thompson's big speed boat and ran over to the mainland.

"I went to your office to look up the people in Thompson's house. I sent a number of telegrams, specified that the answers were to be delivered in your care, and returned to the island. I had a very unpleasant scene with Thompson when I got back. I'm telling you all this because I'm not in his pay. I don't much care if you publish the facts. I'm going to find out who killed that woman and if Thompson did it, I'll send him to the chair."

"You've been here since yesterday noon and you haven't learned a damn thing," remarked Duffy. "How long do you think she had been dead when you saw her?"

"The island doctor said at least twelve hours."

"Longer than that."

"What do you mean?" cried Brady.

"Was she dressed when you saw her?"

"She had on a silver nightgown."

"She was naked when she was murdered."

"**HOW THE DEVIL** do you know?"

"It's no wonder you found no clues in the bedroom, Jack. She was killed on the roof of the Nudist Club late yesterday afternoon."

Duffy laughed to see the eyes of the detective popping from his face.

"She was moved to the house under cover of darkness," he said.

"Where do you get your information?"

Duffy chuckled. "I haven't been here two hours and I've beaten the stuffing out of you."

But Brady was squeezing his arm.

"Damn you, give up," he growled.

"I wormed it out of a young woman who owns a speed boat. I climbed on the boat when I dropped off the steamer. I was drying my clothes when she got aboard. She was at the club when they found Mrs. Thompson. She promised to keep it quiet. When she found I was a reporter she pushed me off the boat. Threw my clothes in after me, damn her."

"Did you get her name?"

"No."

"Would you know the boat?"

"Why, I guess so. I'd know her. She can't get off the island any more than the rest of us."

"Why should Thompson conceal the fact that she was killed at the Nudist Club? Why try to make me think she was murdered in her room?"

"Why hire you at all if he was covering it up?"

Brady nodded vehemently. "I'll find out. Nobody's

making a monkey out of me. Find that girl, Bill, and hold her. Phone me at Thompson's."

"But the phones are out."

"Only long distance. Be very careful. If you're recognized they'll lock you up. And above all keep away from the Nudist Club. I'll meet you at six this evening, sooner, if you locate the girl."

Brady rose. "I'll be getting back. There's something very weird going on here. Something deeper than this killing. By God, I'll find out what it is!"

"Sure, I'll probably be able to tell you."

Brady shook the newspaper man's hand.

"If it turns out that your dope is correct," he said, "you'll have this exclusive."

Duffy put his tongue in his cheek.

"You're going to give me my own scoop," he jeered. "Thanks for everything, Jack."

He gazed satirically after the hulking, retreating form.

"Keep away from the Nudist Club, eh? When this story breaks it's going to need pictures. And I'll get them to the mainland tonight if I have to swim. Hires Brady, puts up this frame on him and fires him. Wants his wife's murderer caught and don't want anybody to catch him. Find that girl so lunkhead Brady can talk to her. Well, when I find her, I'll have a few words to say to her myself."

The sun was hot as Bill walked toward the head of the pier. Having lost his hat and not being one of those daring youths who defy sunstroke by going bareheaded, he stepped into a shop and bought himself a light felt and shoes and stockings.

Tomorrow the tale of the murder at the Nudist Club

would break. The wife of King Tom of Santa Rosalita killed by nudists. A nudist herself. Hardly a member of the Club but a well known figure. Film stars, famous artists, writers, society women. If he could get inside the place and take a few pictures! It must be done now. Tomorrow the Club would be closed, all approaches to it guarded.

4

PEEKING INTO EDEN

DUFFY STARTED UP Canyon Avenue, his pace growing slower as the grade became more steep. For a while the street was lined with cottages closely huddled, and these were replaced by more impressive villas set back from the street, their lawns guarded by stucco walls. After awhile, he left trees and homes behind and climbed through an arid rocky region upon which the sun beat down mercilessly.

Bill began to puff and felt obliged to remove his coat, though his shirt was rumpled and wrinkled as a result of its sea bath and unironed drying.

Up ahead he saw a high white wall, beyond which was the red-tiled parapet of the Nudist Club. It was located upon a mesa several hundred yards in length and width. Beyond it and on either side were high hills.

It looked to Duffy as if this were going to be a hard nut to crack and he had no nut cracker with him.

"Case of marching up the hill and then marching down again, I reckon," he remarked to himself mournfully. "Now how the devil am I going to get over that wall?"

From the airplane picture he was aware that there were spacious grounds about the club house, stretches of thick green turf as carefully tended as the greens of a golf course, winding paths of soft sand for tender naked feet, a large artificial pond, shade trees brought full grown by ship from the mainland. In fact it was a garden of Eden for a lot of sophisticated Adams and Eves who wanted to combine a thrill with a tan.

There was no sense in approaching the entrance to the establishment. He would have to work around to the rear and trust to luck for a chance to get over the wall, which, most likely, was protected by broken glass imbedded in concrete.

He left the road immediately and began to work towards the left of the establishment.

Presently he came to gulch which was quite deep and seemed to afford a way of approach unseen from the modern Garden of Eden. He stumbled along its rocky bottom for some distance, and finally became aware that he had reached the Nudist Club, for a high white wall loomed above him on the right.

Duffy was ten or twelve feet below the foot of the wall and fully twenty feet below its top, and the side of the gulch was so steep he couldn't reach the wall anyway.

The thing looked hopeless, but he decided to keep on. The deep little canyon might feather out further along. He might find a high rock close to the wall which would help him surmount it.

After proceeding several hundred yards, during which the gulch grew narrower and deeper, he saw at the right a two foot aperture.

It might be the lair of a bear or a mountain lion but, as he had never heard of wild animals on Santa Rosalita Island, Duffy crawled through the opening. He found himself in a concrete lined tunnel about two feet wide and six feet high. It led upward. He lighted a match.

The tunnel continued beyond the range of the flickering light, and Duffy, with a grunt of surprise and satisfaction, followed it.

He came presently to a place where it divided. A second match did not help him to decide which to follow so he took the left on speculation. Presently he became aware that it was slippery under foot; a third match revealed a trickle of water. He whistled comprehendingly.

The pond of the Nudist Club was artificial, no doubt, with a concrete bottom, and occasionally required cleaning out. This was a water conduit in which he found himself. Up above was a huge pipe through which the water of the pool emptied into the conduit and finally ran down the gulch. And, if it happened to be the time for emptying the pool, Mr. Bill Duffy would be in a bad way.

He retraced his steps until he came to the place where the tunnel had divided; then he tried the right fork. He had followed this only a short distance when he came up against a blank wall. He struck another match. There was an iron ladder fastened to the wall and above a trapdoor. He went up the ladder and pushed against the trap. It immediately opened, and bright sunlight poured through. In a second Mr. Duffy was out of the tunnel and standing in a small room, obviously used as a storeroom by the Nudist Club.

"And what do you know about this?" inquired Bill triumphantly.

THERE WERE WINDOWS high in the wall on either side. Small windows. Duffy pulled a packing case underneath one of them, climbed on it and then he could see out. He looked upon a wide lawn of deep green grass. Beyond it was the pond, which was circular and a hundred and fifty feet in diameter, with a row of palm trees on the further side. He craned his neck and saw at the right a tennis court, beyond which was a high hedge. Looking to the left, he saw an iron stake in the ground with a lot of horseshoes scattered about it. But nowhere on the grounds of the Nudist Club did he spy a single nude of either sex.

"What's the matter with them?" growled Bill Duffy. "Why don't they come out and get the morning sun the way they ought to? Well, probably it's too early."

He sat down on the packing case, drew forth his camera and inspected it.

"Just my luck," he muttered, "if nobody came out today except some fat women."

It was hot in the storeroom, however, and time dragged. Presently, he heard faintly, high-pitched girlish laughter. The hunter's gleam came into his eye and he climbed again on the packing box and peered out.

Glory be! There were young women out there. Over near the edge of the pond were two girls, slender, graceful nymphs; one was blond and one was dark; they were standing about twenty feet apart, tossing a heavy medicine ball at each other. They were tossing it, but rarely catching it, and they squealed with laughter each time they muffed a throw.

Bill lifted his camera and suddenly felt himself getting as red as a lobster.

The kids thought they were alone. He felt like Peeping Tom of Coventry looking at a couple of Lady Godivas, except that Lady Godiva was sheathed in her long golden hair and neither of these dryads had long hair. His offense was greater than Peeping Tom's. No, it wasn't, for Godiva went forth nude for a noble purpose and the Lord blinded Peeping Tom for peeking at her; while this pair were sporting round out there for pure devilment and other nudists could look at them and they wouldn't give a hoot. Serve them right if he took their pictures.

The trouble was that they were too far away.

"Why don't you come nearer to the camera," he complained. "Damn it, this won't show anything."

Suddenly, one of the bare young maidens screamed something, whereupon both of them threw themselves flat on their stomachs on the grass. A second later there swam into his vision a tall, gray-haired man, who rushed across the lawn, turned sidewise as he passed the girls and plunged into the pool, swimming towards the center with lusty strokes.

"A swell lot of nudists you are," sneered Bill Duffy. "Covering up, the whole lot of you. Great Jumping Jiminy Moses!"

The blond girl had arisen and was walking directly towards him and his camera and she didn't even have a fig leaf. And to the utter consternation of Bill Duffy it was Iris, the woman he had loved and lost, the one who had married the lieutenant-commander under an arch of swords, with a wedding dress on six yards long. It would serve her right if he took her picture and published it with her name under it.

Instead of doing so, however, Mr. Duffy jumped off the packing case and swore softly but at length. While Duffy had his vices, he was ultra-conventional regarding modesty, and Iris had shocked him horribly. While it was true that she didn't know that the man she had jilted was peeking at her through the storehouse window, she was out there naked. And that old scoundrel with the white hair was within seeing distance and there probably were a lot more old satyrs leering from various parts of the ground.

His ears suddenly were intrigued by the sound of voices near him. Apparently the partition between the storeroom and the next room was very thin, because he could hear a man and woman talking and distinguish what they said.

"Brady threw a scare into old Tom," said a woman. "He refuses to leave, won't take a fee, and says he'll find out who killed Mona, no matter what obstacles are placed in his way."

"Of all men in the world to bring to this island," said a male voice. "I gave Tom a piece of my mind."

"Can't he be forced to leave?" she asked.

"You can't frighten him. He's been shot and stabbed a dozen times and come back for more. What was that?"

"Brady," she exclaimed. "He's in the storeroom!"

DUFFY IN HIS excitement had leaned forward and the packing case, which was empty, tipped over with a crash. A hand turned the knob of the storeroom door. It was locked. A key was thrust into the lock. Duffy lifted the trapdoor, leaped into the tunnel and allowed the door to drop with a bang. As fast as he could, he ran in the dark through the tunnel, bumping from one side to another in his haste. He heard the trap lifted behind him and the plop of somebody landing on the tunnel floor, and he ran even faster.

Crash, boom, boom, crash.

Four shots from a revolver. In that narrow concrete

passage they sounded like explosions from a cannon. At the first shot Duffy dropped flat on his stomach.

His murderous pursuer came on. Bill squeezed himself against the right hand wall, acutely conscious that there were two more bullets in the weapon. There wasn't room for the runner to pass. It would have to be a fight to the death in the dark.

He got to his knees and then a rapidly moving body collided with him. His arms wrapped round a pair of naked thighs, and he flung the enemy to the floor with great force. Another shot burst from the revolver with a deafening roar; then Duffy was feeling for his assailant's throat. There was no resistance. He was out cold; had landed on the back of his head on the cold concrete, no doubt. Warily Bill felt for the face. His hand touched a mass of soft hair. With an ejaculation of astonishment, he ran his fingers across the face and neck. A woman! A stark naked woman had pursued him, had had every intention of killing him. A naked woman with a revolver in her hand!

"I'll have a look at you, sister," he muttered, and he fumbled for a match. An inveterate smoker—he didn't have a match. And he heard more footsteps in the tunnel behind him. The other person in the next room was approaching rapidly.

Duffy felt for her hands, but her revolver had gone and he had no time to look for it. He scrambled to his feet and took to his heels. A minute later he crawled through the exit and sped down the gulch, keeping a careful watch behind lest somebody emerge from the tunnel entrance and take a pot shot at him.

"A dame!" he muttered. "A dame with no clothes on.

And with a gat. 'Sure Shot Sal,'—no,—'Nudist Nan, the she-wolf of Santa Rosalita.' And I didn't even get a squint at her.

"Well, here's a hot one for Jack Brady!"

5

BEAUTIFUL YOUNG NUDIST

IT'S ALL IN the point of view. Bill Duffy, as an editor, had had no patience with camera men who returned with nothing important on their plates. Having turned camera man, he had fled from the Nudist Club without a picture. He could have snapped Iris—Iris was probably the only woman in the world he would not have snapped. Hating her already, he hated her more for that.

On the other hand, he had learned something important. The place was a hang-out for criminals—naked criminals. Nudists with revolvers. And they were horribly worried because Jack Brady was on the island. This pair, no doubt, had killed Mona Thompson. Yet they had had the impudence to give Tom Thompson, husband of the murdered woman, a piece of their mind. And Duffy hadn't had a look at either of them.

He left the gulch and walked down the road. He had lost his new hat and the sun was fiery. He perspired freely. He had a grouch.

Just as he was at his grouchiest, as he was passing a cottage on the outskirts, somebody said, "Hello."

He looked up and saw the girl of the speed boat. She had

a sweater on over her bathing suit and she was leaning on a whitewashed stone wall. She was smiling at him pleasantly.

"You retrieved your clothes, I perceive," she remarked.

"No thanks to you," he said grumpily.

She giggled. "You were so cocky. And you had no business on my boat. And I was mad because you wormed something out of me which I should have kept to myself."

"Don't mention it," he growled.

"Have you been up to the Nudist Club?"

"Maybe."

"I bet you didn't get in," she jeered.

While Bill hated women, this one was exceptionally pretty and she knew things which would be useful to him. She was a member of the Club and might be persuaded to tell him the names of some of the prominent members. And, maybe she could get him into the place. He grinned at her.

"I'll forgive you for chucking me overboard," he stated. "Do you live in this house?"

"Yes."

"Could you give me a drink of water?"

"I gave you a drink, didn't I?"

"All right. Rub it in."

She opened a gate in the wall.

"Come on in," she invited. "My sister is at the beach and I might as well talk to you as nobody."

She led the way across a small garden, mostly cactus, and they came to a cool porch on which were comfortable wicker chairs, covered with chintz and a Gloucester hammock. Being tired, Bill immediately threw himself on the hammock.

"Do sit down," she said, laughing. "Would you like a nice long iced limeade?"

"Despite what I know of your character," he replied, "I begin to like you."

He observed with approval her slim, golden brown limbs as she strode toward the house entrance. In five minutes or less she returned with two tall glasses.

"I ventured to put a small quantity of gin in them," she informed him.

"I hate liquor but I wouldn't put you to the trouble of throwing this away," he said with a grin. "Look here, can you take me into the Nudist Club?"

"Certainly not."

"You're a member. Why not take in a guest?"

"According to the rules, the names and information regarding all guests must be submitted to Mr. Thompson for approval."

"That's all right. I'll give you a pedigree."

"No newspaper man is admitted under any circumstances."

"Do you know what I think?" he said in a surly tone. "I think that any girl who would parade around with nothing on hasn't got any sense of decency."

SHE LAUGHED GAYLY. "Now, in my opinion, any person who sees wrong in appearing as nature made us is lewd and lascivious."

"That goes for the whole male sex."

The girl seated herself and crossed her naked thighs.

"Nature, young man," she said blandly, "made no provision for clothing. To wear clothes is an affront to nature. Garments came into vogue when people moved into cool climates. They put them on to keep them warm and discarded them freely when the weather was not cold. Right minded people think nothing of nudity."

"Will you prove that by taking off what few things you have on now?" Bill asked.

She blushed furiously. "Certainly not, because your warped point of view makes nudeness embarrassing."

"Tell me this. If you want to go round naked, why not do it in your own back yard? Why go and show yourself in front of a crowd of men and women?"

"Because persons who are nudists are not affected by nudity. The fact that they are in the same state makes it of no importance."

"Let it pass. Who found Mrs. Thompson dead yesterday?"

"I don't know."

"Why did they move her to the house and give out that she was killed there?"

"Because, naturally, Mr. Thompson didn't want it known publicly that his wife was a nudist; a scandal would ruin the Club. He sent for this private detective for that reason. He put on the quarantine to keep the murderer from escaping from the island. When the murderer is captured, it won't matter where the crime was committed, will it?"

"It will have to come out at the trial. Besides, how can the detective catch this killer, if he can't investigate the scene of the crime?"

"Well, of course, Mr. Brady has been told everything."

Knowing that Brady had been told nothing and that Thompson and others were eager to get him to drop the case and depart, Duffy said nothing in reply to that statement.

"How come you know so much about what's going on?" he demanded.

"Because I was asleep on the roof. I was the only guest left when the crime was discovered. I talked to Mr. Thompson and he requested me to say nothing."

"Maybe you killed Mrs. Thompson," he said with a grin. "You had the opportunity. Were you on good terms with her?"

Her eyes snapped angrily.

"I'm going to phone Mr. Thompson that you are a newspaper man and violated the quarantine. How dare you insinuate—"

"Oh, heck, you wouldn't hurt a fly. Did you ever see nudists up there walking round with revolvers in their hands?"

"Certainly not."

"Well, I did," he said under his breath. "Listen, I think you ought to have a talk with Jack Brady. What's your name?"

"Gertrude Smith. I don't care to talk with him or anybody. Don't you think you ought to be going?"

"O.K., sister." He rose. "Thanks for the—ahem—limeade."

"How do you expect to get back to the mainland?"

"That's an idea. Will you take me over in your boat?"

"Certainly I won't. I wouldn't dare go to sea in her. Besides, I'm interested in keeping this affair out of the newspapers. And, if you quote me, assuming that you do reach San Diego, I'll deny everything and then where will you be?"

"Tell me about Thompson. Do you like him?"

"Not very much. I liked his wife. She was sweet."

"Why should anybody kill her?"

"It's incomprehensible to me."

"Well, all Brady has to do is to find out who were in the Nudist Club yesterday afternoon; the murderer will be one of those."

"Yes, but which one?"

"I don't know. Good-by."

"What are you going to do this evening?" she inquired as he started for the gate.

"Dodge the town cops."

"If you escape them, drop in."

"Then you're not going to give me away?"

"I should, but I won't."

Duffy continued down the canyon. This, he thought was an attractive girl. To be sure, being a nudist, she was a shameless little hussy; and she undoubtedly was mercenary, greedy, mean and faithless like all the other girls. If he were back in San Diego, where there were things to do—bars, poker games and good stories breaking—he wouldn't give her any of his time.

On the other hand, she probably knew more than she let on regarding the affair, and it wasn't likely that the Thompson policemen who might get wind of his presence on the island would come looking for him up there.

It occurred to him as he approached the beach that Iris was either fatter than of yore or clothes disguised her better.

6

DETECTIVE AND CLIENT

PRIVATE DETECTIVE JOHN Brady was in no mood to admire the beauty of the scenic drive he was taking in one of Thomas P. Thompson's fleet of motor cars. One of the laws of the island prohibited motor cars to tourists or residents, Thompson himself excepted. All residents save Thompson lived within easy walking, horseback or carriage distance of the port, and there were no paved roads on Santa Rosalita, with the exception of that which climbed the mountainside to the peak on which the King resided. Like a King, when Thompson invited guests to his home, he sent his cars to fetch them.

Brady had begun his career as a catcher of criminals in the uniform of the New York police. Having more imagination than the average flatfoot, being a notable fighter and a square shooter, he had risen to the rank of captain when his honesty brought him into contact with a corrupt city administration. He resigned from the force and was invited to join the United States Secret Service.

In a few years, having married and started to raise a family, he found it impossible to carry on upon Federal wages and had set up in New York as a private detective.

He had bulldog tenacity and a gift for guessing how

criminals would act under given circumstances by putting himself in their place. He got results and built up a reputation for honesty. There was a fanatic streak in him—hatred of crime and criminals. He was ready to lay down his life to right a wrong.

As the car swung around curves and up grades Brady was trying to figure out why Thompson had gone to the trouble of bringing him from Los Angeles to deceive him. If he wanted his wife's killer captured why conceal the place and circumstances under which the beautiful young woman had perished?

While Jack would scoff at the notion that he was psychic, he had sensed an undercurrent of uneasiness as soon as he set foot in the Thompson residence.

Thompson's attitude had been hostile from the beginning. His son and his beautiful young wife had resented his presence.

Only the Sterling woman, whose status in the household was equivocal, had been at all cordial. Owen Overman, the novelist, had looked down his nose at him. Sized him up as a thick-headed flatfoot.

Brady did not doubt Duffy's statement that the girl had been slain at the Nudist Club instead of in her bedchamber. It explained a number of things which had seemed queer to him.

He had jumped into the car with the intention of having a showdown with Thompson and throwing a scare into him, but he had already changed his mind. When they called the fellow King Tom, it was no figure of speech. While the island was officially a part of a huge rural California County, it was fifty miles from the mainland. It had its own police force, health department and port control. All its officials were tenants and employees of Thompson.

Thompson could declare a quarantine, cut the cable to the mainland and be certain that nobody on the mainland would bother him—for a reasonable length of time, anyway. If he became angry with Brady he could deport him and prevent him from returning to the island. And, if he wanted to protect his wife's murderer, no County authority would prevent him from doing so.

Jack decided that Thompson would not have sent for him unless he intended to use him to capture the murderer. Between the time of his summons and his arrival, the King had changed his royal mind. Why? Because there was some reason which made the capture of the killer less important than it had been.

Was it that Thompson had discovered that his son had slain Mrs. Thompson?

It was possible. Was there some other interest which made it desirable that the killer should not be found? If so, what was it?

Whatever the reason, Brady proposed to capture the murderer of the young woman.

Eight hundred feet above the sapphire sea the car arrived at a great wrought-iron gate in an eight foot stone wall; the gate swung open by means of a crank operated from within the gate keeper's lodge.

The machine moved up a steep driveway, rolled past gardens set in wide terraces, and drew up in front of a huge white structure, which resembled a resort hotel more than it did a home.

Brady alighted and went up three red stone steps to a

broad porch which ran the length of the house, considerably more than a hundred feet.

He had chosen his role, that of a boob. He would conceal the information he had received, continue to snoop about the house, question the inmates and servants and permit Thompson to believe he had no suspicion that all was not as it had been set before him.

At the east end of the porch he espied Thomas P. Thompson and proceeded to join him.

THOMPSON WAS AN exceedingly large man, so broad that at first glance he belied his height of six feet two. He had iron-gray hair, bushy black eyebrows, a big broad nose, and a large mouth with thick lips. He had heavy lids over pale blue eyes. His chest measurement must have been fifty, his waist more than that. He was seated beside a low table, his white flanneled legs stretched straight out. In his right hand he held a tall highball glass and his hand was so enormous that it almost concealed the glass.

He thrust out his under lip as he gazed upon the detective.

"Brady," he said, "I'm raising the quarantine tonight. I have radioed the murder of my wife to the County authorities. I've given you twenty-four hours and you've made no progress. You can take the evening boat, or, if you insist, I'll send you back to Los Angeles by plane."

Brady met his eyes squarely and Thompson's were first to shift.

"I find this situation queer, Mr. Thompson," he said sternly. "It looks to me as though you were afraid I'd stumble onto something else on this island besides a murderer. It looks to me as though you had lost your anxiety to find this killer. I've learned a thing or two. I have certain suspicions regarding the motive and the identity of the murderer of your wife.

"You have? State them."

"I shall make no statement until I have more to go on."

"What the devil do you mean about something besides the murderer? This is a quiet, well managed community. Nothing goes on here which I don't know about. I have come to the conclusion that I was wrong to bring in a private detective. The County authorities are competent—"

"Yesterday you said they were fools and muddlers. You want to get rid of me, don't you?"

"Why, you—" Thompson's voice, ordinarily heavy and deep, lifted in anger.

"Lest I learn something you don't want known, Mr. Thompson."

Thompson's eyes almost closed and the crimson of his face deepened.

"Bah," he said after a few seconds. "Stick around if you like. Fiddle about and give me a bill for your time. The sheriff of the County will be here tomorrow and we'll get some action."

"Very well. I'd like to talk to Miss Sterling. Any objections?"

"Keep a civil tongue in your head when you talk to that young lady. She was Mona's best friend, as I've told you. Anyway she's not here. Nobody is here. They're all at the Nudist Club."

"With a death in the house?"

"I see no reason for imprisoning my guests. The sun and air will do them good."

"There was no smallpox, of course."

"Dr. Olden has decided it was chicken pox."

"You own the Nudist Club, Mr. Thompson. Was your wife a member? Did she go there at all?"

"We're all frequenters of the Club. Why not? It's the greatest health—"

"I understand. Your son and his wife, Miss Sterling, and Mr. Overman were in the house when the murder occurred. I have searched their quarters, as you know. Please give me an order on the manager of the Nudist Club to search their lockers."

"WELL, OF ALL the— Why should I do that, Brady?"

"It's possible one of these four persons killed Mrs. Thompson. If they have something to conceal they would not leave the house and leave it behind. If they are naked at the Club, whatever they carried on their persons will be left in their lockers."

Thompson scowled at him and smiled faintly after a few seconds.

"You claim I give you no cooperation," he said. "Well, I loved my wife. I want the killer hanged. I don't want you to go to the mainland insinuating that I am covering up the members of my family. I'll write you an order."

He rose and went into the house. Brady grinned as he looked after him. Thompson was willing to oblige because it appeared evident that the detective had no suspicion that the murder had occurred, not in the house, but at the Nudist Club.

Thompson's son William was a nonentity. Jane, William's wife, was a red-headed, voluptuous looking young woman who had been a film star. Miss Sterling was a beautiful brunette, nearly thirty years old; Overman was a well known novelist. None of them was apparently capable of murder. Their presence in the house on the night of the crime was of no importance. If they had been at the Nudist Club two days ago, that was something different. But he wasn't telling that to Thompson.

"Here you are and much good will it do you," said the owner of the island, returning and handing him a note. "I've ordered a car for you. I presume you wish to go immediately."

"Thank you, Mr. Thompson."

"Don't mention it." He grinned. "You'll have to strip if you want to go inside the Club."

"Do you?"

"Certainly."

"When were you there last?"

"Eh? Day before yesterday."

"Was Mrs. Thompson there?"

"Yes. What do you want to know for?"

"Oh, no reason."

Under his beetling brows Thompson gazed at him suspiciously. At the moment the car arrived.

7

A DETECTIVE GOES NUDIST

THOMPSON'S CAR SPED up the canyon avenue which Bill Duffy had climbed so painfully and drew up before the portal in the high white wall of the Nudist Club. Brady descended, dismissed the car and rang the bell. An unseen person opened a peep-hole and inspected the visitor.

"I have a letter of introduction from Mr. Thompson to the manager, Mr. Hopkins," said the detective.

"Let me have it, please."

Brady thrust the note through the opening. After a couple of minutes the door opened and he found himself in a covered passage twenty feet long which led directly into the clubhouse.

"I am Mr. Hopkins," said the person who had admitted him. "Pleased to make your acquaintance."

Brady shook hands with a clean shaven individual with a peculiar pallor. He made a note that the club manager didn't appear to take advantage of his opportunities to bathe his body in the health-giving rays of the sun.

They passed into a charming reception room, of which the only distinguishing feature was that it was without windows and was artificially lighted.

"I presume you wish to look about," said the manager,

who wore a blue blazer with brass buttons and white flannel trousers. "Mr. Thompson tells me to put myself completely at your service."

"That's right."

"I trust you will not affront our members by appearing with—er—ordinary dress. One is only conscious of nudity if others wear garments."

Jack was inspecting the room. Opposite the entrance were two doors, one marked "Ladies" and the other "Gentlemen."

Mr. Hopkins smiled broadly. "Undressing rooms. I'll assign you a locker."

"Are there any ladies in the ladies' room?"

"No, sir. Everybody is out in the sunlight."

"Take me in there, please."

Hopkins looked startled. "I say—really—"

"If you don't think that letter means what it says you are at liberty to phone Mr. Thompson."

"There's a maid in there."

"Send her away, please."

"Very well," said the man sullenly. He disappeared through the men's room and reappeared a moment later from the ladies' room.

"All clear," he reported stiffly.

Jack found himself in a large room lined with five foot lockers with doors of steel. On each door there was a name plate.

"Please open the lockers of Miss Sterling and Mrs. William Thompson," he said curtly.

"I—I can't do that, Mr. Brady."

"I was sent here to search the belongings of these ladies

Over near the house he saw two club
members—a man and a woman

by Mr. Thompson. I am a detective engaged by him to investigate the crime at the Castle."

"But these are his family, his friends—" protested the manager.

"You heard what I said. And if you mention to any of the ladies that their effects have been searched, you'll find yourself out of employment."

"Very well," said the manager dolefully.

"Make sure that nobody enters while I am at work, please."

"Yes, sir. I'll fetch the master keys."

It was most unlikely that guests at the Castle who had anything to conceal would have left it in their quarters knowing a detective was prowling about. But having left the Nudist Club locker room in costumes of Adam and

Eve, they had presented Mr. Brady with an opportunity such as seldom is vouchsafed to a criminal investigator.

"Open Miss Sterling's locker," Jack commanded when Hopkins had returned with the pass-key.

"I do this under protest, Mr. Brady."

"I note your protest," said Jack dryly.

Miss Sterling had worn few clothes. There were a pair of tiny slippers in the bottom of her locker, a pair of sheer silk hose; on a hook, a brassiere, and white flannel skirt and closely knit white sweater. No underwear. It couldn't have taken the young lady more than half a minute to disrobe. **ON THE SHELF**, however, was a white leather bag of which Brady possessed himself. Taking a stool, he proceeded to inspect it at his leisure.

It contained a mirror, a bunch of keys, and in an inner purse, a folded twenty-dollar bill and some small change. And there were two folded letters.

He drew, without scruple, the enclosure from the first. It was a notice from a modiste in New York that, if she did not receive an immediate remittance, she would turn over Miss Sterling's account to her lawyers.

"Poor kid," he muttered and replaced the threatening letter.

He drew forth the other enclosure, observing that the envelope was unstamped and was addressed simply to Miss Sterling.

There was a page of writing in a bold hand.

DARLING:

I assure you you can't believe the evidence of your eyes.
Mona is nothing to me, at least no more. I implore you to

give me a chance to really talk to you. Don't condemn me unheard. I've never believed the things they say about you. Be as fair to me.

The letter was unsigned but Brady was certain that it had been written by Owen Overman.

These two hangers-on in the Thompson household were interested in each other. He had sensed that at dinner last night. No doubt he had flirted with the young and frivolous wife of the millionaire and Lida Sterling had resented it. Of course Overman might not have written this letter but Brady would have bet on it. He thrust it into his pocket.

The manager was agitated. "You can't keep that letter. Its loss will be discovered." Brady silenced him with a glance.

The detective next turned his attention to the effects of Mrs. William Thompson, who was the former film star, Jane Jerome. There was a vial containing white pellets which he examined with some interest and a folded letter several months old which he read. It was brief, astounding and none of his business, so he replaced it. It was a passionate effusion from a person who signed himself Carl, but wrote on the letterhead of Karl Klauson, the motion picture director. It implored her to escape to the mainland for another exquisite week-end.

It appeared that the young son of Tom Thompson was being victimized. Married for his money, of course. What could he expect? But it had no bearing on the case in hand and it was up to him to forget he had ever read it. But what an idiot the woman was to carry such an explosive in her purse!

"Finished," he informed the manager.

"Thank God," ejaculated Hopkins.

"Here, I mean," stated Jack, smiling broadly. "I'm going to have a look in the men's locker room now, if you please."

SEARCH OF THE lockers of the two men revealed nothing of the slightest interest and Brady knocked on the inner door, which Hopkins instantly opened.

"Are you through?" he asked.

"With my search. I should like to inspect the place, if you please."

"You'll have to undress, sir. Otherwise I cannot admit you."

Brady hesitated.

"This is the rummest go," he muttered. "O.K. If they can stand it, I can."

Hopkins opened a locker. Brady removed his garments reluctantly until he stood forth as Nature had sent him into the world.

"Let's go," he proposed.

"I am on duty, sir. You don't mind wandering about alone?"

The detective shook his head. "I'll make out, I reckon." He wanted to inspect the place without the shrewd eyes of Hopkins on him. He didn't like the looks of Hopkins. The fellow had a pasty complexion and evasive eyes and in Brady's opinion he had a past.

The manager unlocked the inner door; Brady entered a rubber tiled lounging room equipped with cushioned chairs and divans. To his relief it was empty. Beyond the lounge was a small dining room, containing two long tables set for luncheon. It also was empty. He passed through it, pushed open a door and looked into a pantry. Two nude waiters were at work there. Brady chuckled.

He returned to the lounge and ascended a flight of stairs which led directly to the roof. When he pushed open the door at the top of the stairs he drew back with an exclamation of horror. There were people on the roof, men and women stretched on rows of cots, taking the sun in their birthday suits. Most of them had their eyes closed and nobody lifted a head to gaze upon the new arrival.

"Got to be done," muttered Brady. He stepped boldly out upon the roof. This, it seemed, was the scene of the murder of Mrs. Thompson.

ABOUT THE TIME that Brady leaned his arms upon the parapet of the roof of the Nudist Club, Bill Duffy was flying down a dark conduit pursued by a naked woman. This Jack was to learn about later.

The sun roof was about sixty feet long by thirty feet broad. It contained twenty cots, half of which were occupied. There were steamer chairs, and shaded hammocks for those who had had enough of the burning rays which already were heating the blood of the detective.

Assuming that Mrs. Thompson had been lying here alone, semi-somnolent, it would be an easy matter for the strangler to overpower her.

There were questions he would like to ask. Hopkins, no doubt, had officiated in the removal of the dead woman to her home under cover of darkness.

He wondered why Thompson had changed the apparent place of the crime. Surely not to save the reputation of the resort. Even though he owned and profited from the place, he would not risk the escape of the murderer for any such reason. Thompson was a very rich man and the revenues of the Club must be apparently unimportant. There was a deeper reason. A sinister one.

As any inquiry he made would undoubtedly be reported to King Tom by his faithful employees, this was not the time to make them. Find out what the island owner really was covering up, and the motive and perpetrator of the killing might be revealed. There was the girl Duffy had spoken to who must be interviewed. He wouldn't show his hand yet.

As the sun bathers lay like the dead, his self consciousness left him and he gazed with interest upon the grounds of the establishment. A landscape artist had performed a miracle upon this desert mesa.

Grim bare hills frowned down upon an exquisite oasis. In the center of this park of a dozen acres was a large lake, the surface of which was rippled by the heads of half a dozen swimmers.

Beyond it was a cluster of royal palms. In the foreground was a wide stretch of thick grass upon which nude human figures moved or lay stretched out motionless. There were avenues of high shrubs which gave shade that was pleasant, beds of gorgeous flowers. There was an archery course upon which several men and women were at play.

Many of the nudists wore dark glasses and their noses and upper lips were whitened like clowns in a circus. He was unable to identify any of the guests at King Tom's Castle.

He saw tennis courts which were in use, and there was a baseball game going on. The players were using a soft ball and cricket bats. On the grounds and roof there must have been half a hundred people. Aside from the fact that they were fully exposed to the view of one another, their play was like that of innocent children. It was exceedingly likely that the murderer of Mrs. Thompson was among them.

Brady's back, unaccustomed to exposure, was getting very hot. A young woman rose from a cot at the end of the roof and walked leisurely and gracefully in his direction. The detective took fright and sped down the stairs to the lounge. A nude attendant rang a bell; Hopkins went to the locker room and opened his locker.

"Please phone the Castle to send a car," he said as he drew on shirt and shorts with great satisfaction.

8

MR. DUFFY DOES HIS DUTY

WILD WILLIAM DUFFY continued on down the canyon which had become a village street. He had almost reached the boulevard when his conscience spoke to him sharply.

He had no pictures. And if he didn't get them today, no pictures of the nudists at play would ever be taken. The club members would hardly gambol on the green and in the water with policemen and sheriff's officers about the place, as they would be when the paper published his story in the morning.

And, while that girl had said that she wouldn't betray him, she might have phoned the local police that there was a reporter at large, in which case Thompson's cops would nab him on the boulevard. Both duty and discretion suggested having another try at the Nudist Club.

If he could snap a few nudes, lie low until darkness, steal a speed boat and risk the trip to the mainland, he would have a story which would make the job of Managing Editor Duffy secure for another couple of months.

While he stood on the sidewalk cogitating, a motor car honked and a big touring car rushed by him at high speed. He had a glimpse of Detective Jack Brady in the back seat.

Brady seemed deep in thought; anyway, he didn't see his friend Bill Duffy.

Bill's ire rose. So he had to keep away from the Nudist Club, but Jack had been up there getting an eyeful. He might just as well have taken his friend in with him.

Duffy climbed the steep grade once more. He peered over the wall when he reached the residence of the young and friendly blonde. The girl wasn't visible. Most likely she had gone to the Club. It would serve her right if he snapped a picture of her. Teach her the value of modesty. Well, maybe he wouldn't snap her, but he might get a good look at her.

He perspired freely and finally took his coat off and carried it on his arm. Presently he turned aside into the ravine which ran alongside the grounds of the club. He grew more and more warm.

It was most unlikely that the lady with the gun would be lurking in the underground passage. In all probability they had concluded that the intruder wasn't in the least likely to return.

As he arrived at this conclusion he reached the hole in the side of the gulch which gave admittance to the conduit. He stopped, entered a few feet, and bumped against a steel door. It was a circular door about three feet in circumference and it caused Bill Duffy to swear eloquently.

He crawled out. Being horribly tired, he sat down on the ground and looked up at the wall of the Club wistfully. Although he was at the bottom of a gully, he was several hundred feet above the village. There was an excellent view of it from the Club, and he also could see the great white structure which King Tom had built for himself on top of a mountain. Not having eaten since 6 a.m., he was hungry. He looked at his watch which had been in his trousers pocket when the blonde threw the trousers overboard.

It had stopped. He judged by the sun that it was about noon. At the end of fifteen minutes Bill was still hot but less fatigued. He was about to get on his feet when he became aware of a grating sound behind him.

The steel door was being opened. He glanced wildly around. The canyon feathered out a couple of hundred feet above. If he started down, he would be seen by whoever was using the passage as an exit. A sizable boulder was a dozen feet away. It was above the passage exit, and he made himself small behind it. The grating sound ceased and there emerged from the hole a man fully clothed, who started down the ravine without a glance in the direction of the boulder.

Duffy had a good look at the fellow. He was a nondescript person of middle height, slender, with brownish hair under a golf cap. He wore a white sweater and dark pants. He stepped out briskly.

BEFORE HE HAD gone a hundred feet Bill had popped into the hole and was feeling anxiously for the door. As he had hoped, it was open. He started forward cautiously, feeling his way, muttering disgustedly because he was still without matches.

After a time he came to the place where the passage divided and he turned to the left. Presently he reached the end, stood on the ladder and tried to push up the trap door; apparently it led into the storehouse from which he had fled an hour or more back. It did not budge. It was bolted in place.

Well, it would have been too good to be true. It looked as if he were foiled again. Disgruntled, he retreated until he came to the fork. While there wasn't much sense in following the other passage, which must end under the middle of the big swimming pool, he might as well become familiar with it. He didn't see why they had this elaborate underground passage way. An ordinary iron pipe would do for emptying the pool.

He did not think to count his steps until he had proceeded some distance, and at the end of several minutes he bumped into a concrete wall. There wasn't a ray of light and his eyes hadn't become familiar with the darkness—there has to be some slight illumination to make that possible.

Feeling round carefully and finding himself in a *cul-de-sac,* he turned about and retraced his steps. At the end of a few score yards he bumped his head against a steel or iron object. Reaching up, he took hold of the bottom of a ladder, which protruded about a foot from the roof of the passage.

Pulling himself up on the bottom rungs, he felt about and discovered that the ladder was fastened to the side of a circular shaft. With some difficulty he stood upon the bottom rung and felt above his head. Touching nothing, he continued to climb. After a few feet his outstretched hand touched the bottom of a manhole cover.

While it might let the lake in if he succeeded in opening it, he decided that if the lake was above it, the weight of water would prevent him from budging it. He pushed. It resisted. He climbed higher, got his back against it and shoved. It yielded. Suddenly the manhole was flooded with dazzling sunlight. He peered through. A few feet from

him was a thick hedge about seven or eight feet tall. Bill
pushed open the cover and climbed out. He was within the
grounds of the Nudist Club! He lay flat and reconnoitered.
Over near the house he saw two club members—a man
and a woman—but their backs were toward him. There was
nobody else in sight. All at lunch, no doubt.

A man wearing clothes and carrying a camera would
cause a sensation in this place. Bill carefully replaced the
manhole cover, on top of which was a layer of sod; and
crawled upon his belly until he was beneath the shrubbery.
There he crouched, like a tiger in his lair. His eyes were
gleaming with triumph. His trusty camera was in his hand.

"Now bring on your nudists," he challenged exultingly.

Pretty soon the sun worshipers would finish eating and
begin to stroll about the grounds. Some of them were sure
to drift within range of his camera, which would be their
hard luck.

Bill's plan was simple. He would remain concealed in the
thick shrubbery, snap all and sundry, wait until darkness
came. Then he would escape, either through the manhole
or over the wall. In all probability they had but one watch-
man, who certainly couldn't be everywhere at once.

The taking of people's pictures without their permission is a newspaper practice of long standing, the ethics
of which has always been moot. Snapping persons who
assumed they were assured of their privacy might seem
unfair, but not to Wild William Duffy. Bill considered
nudists fair game. If they objected to being snapped in their
birthday suits, why did they wander around in the open air,
in the presence of persons of both sexes? He didn't have any
more qualms than a hungry lion stalking a deer.

And at the end of half an hour, exponents of the art of nudism came out of the clubhouse and began to wander about.

With a heartless chuckle, Bill snapped Harvey Howard, one of the leading realtors of San Diego. Mr. Howard stood only twenty feet from him, spread out his arms, drew a long breath and gazed rapturously at the sun. That was how Bill took him.

A few minutes later his eyes glittered as a gorgeous red-haired woman moved in his direction with an undulating gait. Her figure was absolutely perfect, in the opinion of the connoisseur in the bushes; when she came closer he muttered excitedly. She was Jane Jerome, the film star who had married William Thompson, son of the millionaire. Click, went the camera.

He secured six pictures, four of them of well known persons. One was a male reformer of San Diego, who had started a movement in that city against mixed bathing a couple of years back. Duffy gloated when he snapped that fellow.

To his surprise, the club members disported themselves most decorously.

Taking it by and large, however, it was one of the most exciting afternoons of his life. He grinned maliciously at grotesque fat women and men with rotund figures but these were in the minority. Most of the nudists were young and well-formed; at least a dozen of the girls were beautiful. And they seemed to take their lack of apparel with extreme nonchalance, which was more than Duffy did.

ALONG ABOUT FOUR o'clock a cold wind came up; the members began to move toward the clubhouse. It was just as well, since Bill had discovered that his spare roll of film, which he had carried in the pocket of his jacket, had been spoiled by sea water. If the film in the camera had also spoiled Bill would commit suicide. He was confident, however, that the leather case had protected the camera.

During this most enjoyable and successful afternoon, Duffy had devoted no thought to the murder mystery. That was Brady's job. He had the story of the death of the young woman, there were photographs of her in the office, and to make things complete he had pictures of nudists and scenes inside the club.

All he had to do was to escape from the place with his camera, run the quarantine, cross the open sea in a small boat and reach San Diego. And he would manage that all right.

He was rather glad that Gertrude Smith had not wandered within range of his camera. While she appeared to think nothing of nudity, Bill thought a picture would be taking unfair advantage. Not that he liked the girl. He didn't like any girls.

The hedge in which he was concealed was very thick, with occasional thorns; since Bill had been forced to lay flat on his stomach, there was considerable pressure of branches against his back and sides. During the period of activity upon the grounds he had submitted to discomfort like a zealous hunter, but now became acutely aware of the disadvantages of his position.

He had time to wonder about the fellow who had left the club via the conduit. Had he returned? If so, how had he obtained entrance to the building, since the trap in the storeroom was locked? Perhaps it would be unbolted at a specified time. Well, that didn't interest Bill—he had secured what he had come after. But why hadn't the man used the proper exit?

The hedge was about fifty feet long and only about six or seven feet in width. In search of comfort, Bill had wriggled back a foot or two, broken off branches which were tickling his face and dug into the soft ground. Nevertheless he found waiting for the sun to set most trying to his patience.

It was getting dusk when he observed a nudist coming from the clubhouse. At that distance he looked like a Negro, but as he approached Bill realized that he was tanned almost chocolate from head to foot. He was enormous. His shoulders were tremendously wide, his chest huge and his arms remarkably developed. He had jet black hair, very curly, black eyes, high cheek bones and a thick neck. His legs were very powerful. He was by far the finest physical specimen on exhibition that day. He went past the hedge to the edge of the swimming pool, plunged in, swam about for a few minutes and came forth, glittering with drops of water.

He came directly toward the hedge and Bill backed into it a little deeper. The fellow looked like an ugly customer, though he was handsome in his way.

The man uttered an expletive. He stooped and inspected the manhole cover, which Bill hadn't troubled to replace exactly as it had been when he pushed it up. He dropped on all fours and fixed it. The hair on his chest was so thick as to suggest fur.

He rose and looked about searchingly. Presently he walked away and the man in the hedge breathed a sigh of relief. A moment later he heard a growl; then he was grasped by the ankles and forcibly dragged from his covert, dragged so swiftly that he could not protect himself from brambles.

LIKE THE OSTRICH, Bill Duffy had assumed he was unobserved because his head was covered. But as he had retreated upon the approach of the giant, his feet and ankles had protruded beyond the rear of the hedge. The nudist had spied a pair of boots and the tops of black socks where boots and socks were forbidden.

A huge hand grasped Bill by the collar and pulled him to his feet. Fierce black eyes stared into his own.

"Detective, eh?" growled the giant. "Snooping, eh? Well, you're through, Mister Detective!" He shifted his grip and with both of his big hands grasped the newspaperman by the throat. He shook him as though he had been a rat. Bill, who was no coward, drove both fists into a naked stomach as hard as steel. A bare leg tripped him. He went over backwards, the giant upon him and the big man set about methodically to choke him to death.

Duffy fought like a mad man, with fists and feet and knees; but he was practically helpless. His wind was cut off. His struggles grew weaker.

There was a roaring sound in his ears. Weird thoughts flashed through his failing brain. He wouldn't be able to call on that girl tonight. And what a story this was, only he wouldn't write it. There would be two murders at the Nudist Club. The eyes staring into his grew as big as saucers. The upper lip of the murderer drew back, showing cruel white teeth. And then his eyes blurred. Everything began to grow black. He was dying.

Suddenly he was freed of the choking grip on his throat.

The giant had spied the camera, which Bill had dropped when he had been lifted to his feet.

The man took his enormous weight from Duffy's body. He stood up and picked up the camera and stared at it. Bill began to come back to life, but he felt very sick and unable to move.

The fellow looked at the camera from all angles and then gazed down upon Bill Duffy.

"You a reporter?" he demanded.

Bill couldn't speak. He managed to nod his head feebly.

"Making pictures of the members, eh?"

"Y-es," whispered Duffy.

The giant dropped the camera to the ground, lifted his right foot and brought it down with all his force upon the machine. It crushed like paper beneath the force of the blow. Bill groaned and hoped the lenses would cut the brute, but they didn't.

"Why didn't you say so?" the man demanded.

Bill felt well enough to sit up.

"You didn't give me a chance," he said bitterly. "That's a seventy-five dollar camera."

"I'm Joe Diblee, the physical instructor," said the giant amiably. "I used to be a wrestler."

"Never heard of you," Duffy said with satisfaction.

Mr. Diblee grinned. "I wrestled under another name. I knew a lot of newspapermen in those days. How did you get over the wall?"

"What do you care?"

"I ain't got nothing against reporters, but you can't sneak in here and make pictures. 'Gainst the rules. You can't wear clothes in here, either."

Bill got upon his feet. Diblee was a slow witted fellow, he thought, stupid like most wrestlers, terrible in battle but good-natured otherwise.

"A fellow has to do what he's told," he said craftily. "I had to get in here or lose my job."

"You got to earn your living like I have," said the recent strangler sympathetically. "Well, I smashed your damn camera. If I take you through the clubhouse the manager will raise hell. Come here."

He grasped Duffy's arm and ran him across the lawn to the wall.

"I'll boost you over," he said. "You better get back to the mainland before King Tom finds out what you tried to put over."

He stooped, Bill climbed on his shoulders and then he rose. Duffy was able to grasp the top of the wall with ease. There was neither broken glass nor wire on it. He swung a leg over.

"Much obliged," he said with a grin. He hung at full length, dropped about four feet and landed on the ground safely. He was about a hundred and fifty feet from the entrance to the place and the ground sloped steeply within a few feet of the wall. He scrambled down until he came to the road and for the second time that day retreated from the Nudist Club, defeated in his purpose. He mourned his camera. He mourned more for the six priceless prints which had been destroyed with it.

9

DEDUCTIONS

ON THE OTHER hand, Duffy had learned something. Diblee was a strangler. Since the killing had taken place at the Nudist Club, and since Diblee made a practice of choking people, it seemed obvious that he had strangled Mrs. Thompson.

A *crime passionel,* that's what it was. This thick-headed giant had fallen in love with the beautiful platinum haired wife of the multi-millionaire, Thomas Thompson. While he was nothing but a paid employee and she was the wife of the owner of the island, he had yearned for her.

Bill got excited thinking about it. What a story! Different from any love tragedy ever published in a paper. Such a man would see such a woman only from afar in ordinary romances, but he was the physical instructor of the Nudist Club and she was a beautiful nudist.

Perhaps she had flirted with the poor brute. Lured him on and then had told him frankly that she could not respond to his love. Sneered at him. Laughed at him. Told him he was only a servant.

And in the little mind of the big man came the lust for revenge. If he could not have her, nobody would have her. He would kill her with his bare hands.

He had watched his opportunity and it had come the day before yesterday. The poor woman had fallen asleep on a cot on the roof. Everybody had gone, save Gertrude Smith, who lay asleep on another cot some distance away.

Softly the great naked brute had crept toward the woman who had scorned him. He stood over her, gloating as he gazed upon her charms of face and form. And then the great hands had closed around her neck.

Back to nature. A cave man killing a cave woman who had turned him down.

Bill knew from experience the strength of those hands. She had not uttered a sound. He had squeezed hard for five minutes, maybe, and when he drew away his hands from her throat she was dead. Then perhaps he had wept and slunk away.

Duffy grew excited as he visualized the crime. Unfortunately he couldn't make a word picture of it for the printed page until the criminal had been arrested for the crime. Well, maybe that could be arranged. He would get hold of Jack Brady, tell him what he had discovered, make the arrest tonight and get the whole story in the morning paper.

No. The managing editor's point of view objected. The report of the murder of the beautiful wife of the owner of Santa Rosalita Island at her husband's Nudist Club was big enough for one day. Save the arrest of the physical instructor to follow up the next day. He would arrange with Brady not to make the arrest until the next morning.

In a brown study he passed the house where Gertrude Smith resided. Suddenly he became aware that an excursion steamer was passing out through the gap in the breakwater. It meant that the quarantine was lifted. There would be no obstacle to his departure. He would hire a big motor boat to take him to San Diego.

Joyfully he hastened his steps. It was a pity he had lost his pictures, but the exclusive story in his possession would put him in right with the publisher.

As he reached Beach Boulevard he decided he ought to phone Jack Brady. The way he was putting things over on that detective was nobody's business. He was entitled to do a little gloating.

He entered a phone booth in a drug store and looked up the number of the Thompson residence. A servant answered.

"I would like to speak to Mr. Brady," he said. "Is he there?"

"Yes, sir. Who shall I say is calling?"

"A Mr. Duffy."

In a moment Brady came on the line.

"Where are you?" he demanded.

"In a cigar store right opposite the pier."

"Wait there. I'll be with you in ten minutes."

The detective hung up. Bill considered. A fast boat would reach San Diego in two and a half or three hours. If he arrived by midnight he would be in ample time for the city edition. After all, Jack was a good guy; since he had his story, he had no objection to helping the poor fellow out. This morning he had told Brady where the murder was committed. Tonight he would tell him who perpetrated the crime. Pretty good for one day.

LIGHTS SUDDENLY BLAZED in the row of lamps which followed the crescent of the beach. They gleamed like jewels on the neck of a beautiful woman. On the harbor scores of gold specks glowed, the lights of pleasure craft at their moorings. High on the mountain sides gleamed the lamps of the island residences.

"I must come here some time and spend my vacation," Bill muttered. "Wonder if that Smith girl lives here all the year round."

Presently the headlights of a motor car appeared down the avenue and approached rapidly. The car stopped at the pier head and Jack Brady descended. He waved to the chauffeur, who continued down the avenue and crossed the street to where Duffy was standing.

"Have you eaten?" he asked casually.

Duffy's stomach suddenly clamored. He hadn't taken nourishment since six that morning and had not been aware until now that he had been fasting.

"No, I'm starving," he said wistfully. "Let's have dinner at that café over the water."

"I was getting ready for dinner at the house. Might have been poisoned, so maybe it's just as well you called up."

"Still unpopular up there?"

"Very," said Jack dryly.

Half a block down they stepped into a café, which was constructed upon an old scow moored to the shore. There was a charming little deck house. Tables were set on the deck, each with a lighted lamp upon it. There were few patrons. The two men secured a table at the rail of the craft and when Brady suggested a sirloin steak, Duffy did not quarrel with the idea.

"Have a showdown with the old so and so?"

"No," said the detective. "I'll learn more by pretending to believe him."

"Learn anything?"

"I've begun to get a line on several of the people staying with Thompson." He chuckled. "I've been at the Nudist Club. The crowd at the house went there today, and while they were sunning themselves I went through their effects in the club lockers."

"It's a lucky thing for you that I decided to take an interest in this case," said Duffy with an exasperating grin. "I was out at the Nudist Club myself—"

"I told you to keep away from there," Brady said angrily.

"I'm not taking orders from you, brother—"

The eyes of the two men clashed and then the detective smiled. "I admit that. The ends of justice don't interest you. You're after sensational news."

"Granted, but I'm further along in clearing up this mess than you are, have a greatly exaggerated notion of your detective ability. These people gave Thompson a piece of their mind for bringing you here. They are so anxious to get rid of you that they'll kill you. One of them darn near killed me because he thought I was Jack Brady."

"And who are these people who give orders to the owner of the island?" Jack demanded eagerly.

"One of them is the murderer of Mrs. Thompson," replied the newspaperman. "Name of Diblee. Physical instructor at the Nudist Club. He had me almost dead when he spied my camera and realized I was a reporter. After that he was quite nice to me, comparatively speaking."

"Begin at the beginning," pleaded the detective. "Never

mind your theories. State facts and I'll make the deductions from them."

"O.K. Immediately after I left you this morning, I started for the Nudist Club with my trusty camera." He related the events of his first visit.

10

A FRUITLESS CALL

"IT'S INCREDIBLE," COMMENTED the detective satirically. "A naked woman fired at you, chased you down this tunnel, and you left her unconscious without getting a look at her."

"I'm telling you. There was another one coming up fast. I had to scram."

"Another woman?" jeered the detective.

"The man this woman had been talking to when I fell off the packing case."

"As you're not working for me, there's nothing I can do about it," Brady said mournfully, "but you shouldn't have fallen off that packing case in the first place. In the next place, if you had to run, you should have carried off your Venus."

"Diana was the Goddess who went around shooting," said Duffy with a chuckle.

"I stand corrected. You should have carried her in your arms until you reached the light. If you could identify that woman I'd be a long way toward finding the murderer of Mrs. Thompson."

"Self preservation is the first law of nature. Besides, I'm a man and this dame was in her birthday suit. I tip you off that you're going to get murdered and in return you bawl me out for not clearing up the case. Anyhow, I'll show you the murderer. I will now tell you about my second visit to the Nudist Club."

"Yes, yes. Would you know this woman's voice?"

"There wasn't anything unusual about it."

"Do you know if she was tall or short, fat or lean?"

"She was well upholstered but not fat. I mean she had an—er—well, she was well padded."

"All the women from the Castle have good figures. This was about half past eleven, you say. Well the guests at Thompson's were all in the Club at that time. Would you know the man's voice?"

"I doubt it."

"I must have been on the roof of the Club when you were running down that passage."

"On the roof? Jack, were you nude?"

The detective colored and his face grew crimson as Duffy rocked with mirth.

"It was the only way I could get in," he protested.

"Will you pose for a picture?" inquired Bill sweetly.

"Get on with your story, darn you."

Brady laid down his knife and fork as Duffy related his adventures in Eden. His eyes narrowed and he scowled in concentration.

"So you see," said Duffy finally, "he thought I was you and he had me almost dead when he saw my camera. After that he became quite sociable and helped me over the wall. He murdered Mrs. Thompson sure as shooting. Crime of passion, as the French put it."

"You say he was a wrestler?"

"He said so."

Jack drew a newspaper clipping from his pocket.

"Does he look anything like this?" he demanded.

"It's him. Arthur Gomez. Where did you get this clipping?"

"Swiped it from your morgue," said the detective with a grin. "It was in the Thompson envelope. Arthur Gomez was the first husband of Mona Thompson. Divorced him in Reno. Thompson paid the costs. I've made inquiries at the house regarding the employees at the Nudist Club. It seems that Mr. Diblee was engaged as physical instructor at the suggestion of Mrs. Thompson. I doubt if Thompson knows that Diblee was the first husband of his wife. What does that suggest to you?"

"Intrigue," said Bill excitedly. "Mona married Thompson for his money but continued to love her former husband. Finds she can't get along without him. So she got him this job, and they meet daily at the Nudist Club. In secret, of course."

"In that case, is it likely that he would murder her?"

"That's right. Well, look here. Thompson discovered the intrigue. He strangled his wife. He sends for you, after setting the stage so you won't have a chance to get the facts. You look dangerous when he meets you, so he wants to get rid of you. It's a cinch Thompson killed his own wife."

"How about that man and woman who said in your presence that they didn't want me on the island?"

Bill scratched his head.

"I forgot that," he mumbled.

"THOMPSON HAD DECIDED to turn the case over to the County authorities," said Brady. "He probably had influence over them and they will accept his dictum. He has lifted the quarantine and restored the *status quo*. As a New York detective I have no standing here. Thompson's attitude is secretly hostile. I insinuated that he was covering something up, that he had changed his mind about catching his wife's murderer and he was forced to tell me to go ahead with my investigation."

"What did he say when you asked him why he concealed the place where the woman was strangled?"

Brady smiled. "Oh, I didn't ask him. I wanted him to think that I was deceived about that. But I'd sure like to meet this couple who discussed me in your hearing. No doubt the man was the same one you saw leaving the place by the conduit. That's a rather remarkable conduit, by the way."

"That's what I thought. As far as I can see, all it's good for is to empty that swimming pool. A big drain-pipe would do that just as well."

"You've been so busy that you haven't found the girl who tipped you that Mrs. Thompson was murdered at the Nudist Club?"

"Oh, I've found her," said Bill. To his annoyance, his cheeks were flushed.

"I want to talk to her."

"Well, I'm invited to call this evening. We won't stay long. I'm going to get to the mainland with my story."

"Hold up the location of the killing as a favor to me."

"I'm being paid by my paper and so far I'm doing all the favors, Jack."

Brady shrugged.

"Have it your own way," he said. "You're making my job more difficult."

He paid the check and Duffy led the way up the canyon road in the direction of the cottage occupied by Gertrude Smith.

"How rich is Thompson, Bill?"

"Supposed to be worth fifty millions. This island is supposed to net him fifty or a hundred thousand a year."

"He has another son, according to your records in the obituary cabinet."

"Yeh. The kid got the grand bounce about a year ago. It was rumored that Thompson caught him paying attention to his beautiful young mother-in-law. He tried to drink up all the booze in San Diego and then vanished off the map. I saw Jane Jerome at the Club this afternoon. Got a swell shot of her, only that big hairy brute Gomez or Diblee smashed my camera."

"Any scandal about her?"

"Not that I know of."

The detective thought of the note in his breast pocket, smiled and said nothing.

"Here we are," announced Duffy. He led the way up the path to the porch of Miss Smith's residence. It was dark and so was the house. He rang but nobody responded.

"Darn her," he said angrily. "She asked me to drop in."

The pair retraced their steps to the Village and separated. Duffy made a deal with the proprietor of a speed boat to take him to the mainland and jumped aboard a motor cruiser called the "Starling."

She was fast and a good seaboat. She left the island at eight. At a few minutes before eleven she tied up at the municipal landing in San Diego. Bill took a taxi to his office.

As his was a morning newspaper there was great activity in the city room at that hour. He paused long enough to order the front page cleared and to ask if the Resalva County officials had given out anything about a murder on Santa Rosalita.

"Not a word," cried the city editor. "Shall I call up the district attorney?"

"Not on your life. I've got the story. Send Jones into my office and I'll give it to him."

He found his secretary at her desk in a corner of his office.

"How is your illness, Mr. Duffy?" she inquired.

"I've recovered temporarily. Go into the morgue and get these envelopes." He scribbled a list of names headed by Thomas P. Thompson. "Now, Jones, let's get busy."

FOR AN HOUR he dictated, the light of enthusiasm in his eyes; then he dismissed Jones and sent for another rewrite man.

"Take these envelopes," he commanded. "Write the life story of Thompson. Have somebody get out all the pictures of Mrs. Thompson, formerly Mona Morgan; also Jane Jerome, now Mrs. William Thompson. Is this a story?"

"I'll say it is."

"There is a telegram here for Mr. Brady," said the secretary. "It came in your care."

She laid the telegram in front of him. Bill eyed it wistfully. He was strongly tempted to open it in hope it would help his story. But Jack trusted him. And, after all, he had a yarn that would excite the nation.

As it was written, it set the murder at Thompson's residence, since King Tom had so stated to Brady. Duffy had only Gertrude Smith's statement that it had occurred at the Nudist Club and she had asserted that she would deny it. Moving the body and concealing the place and circumstances of the crime was a felony for which Thompson was liable. Duffy, functioning now as an editor instead of a reporter, dared not let the paper in for a libel suit from such an important person as the owner of Santa Rosalita.

Since the murder was a *Sphere* exclusive, the story was big enough as things were. Tomorrow, he hoped to be able to prove the fact that the crime had taken place at the Club, which would be a magnificent follow-up.

"Get me a small camera," he commanded his secretary. "Tell the boss I've gone back to Santa Rosalita. Kiss me good-by, in case you never see me again. Hell will break loose when the paper gets on that island."

With another camera, Duffy left the office and returned to the waiting motor cruiser.

"Wake me up when we reach the island," he told the boatman. "Don't know when I'll have another chance to snatch a few winks."

He slept two hours and woke up refreshed. The boatman told him that Santa Rosalita was only ten miles away. As they were approaching the north and uninhabited side, there were no lights to indicate its location.

Time passed. Bill suddenly became aware of a winking light away off to port. He stared. Some vessel was using Morse lights. Bill could read Morse but the letters didn't make sense.

"Using a code," he muttered.

"It's being answered ashore," said the boatman.

He stared shoreward. The village was only a few miles off, a cluster of lights. Directly abeam, on the shore, there was a pin point of light which appeared and disappeared. Bill watched and translated but the message also was in a code.

"Smuggling, I guess," he muttered. "Well, it's none of my business."

A few minutes later the boat slipped into the harbor, darted toward the landing stage for motor craft and Bill Duffy stepped ashore. The village was fast asleep apparently, but as he climbed the steps to the street a uniformed man confronted him.

"Who are you and where are you from?" he demanded.

"San Diego. Nothing concealed about the person, Mr. Officer."

The officer tapped his pockets and grunted.

"O.K.," he said. "Nothing on you. It's suspicious, you coming in at this hour." He peered down at the boat.

"It's me, Dan Knowlton, Tom," called the boatman. "I took this feller to the mainland and back."

Nodding his head, the customs man walked back to his shack at the head of the pier. Bill grinned, recalling the winking lights. It wasn't likely that smugglers would come up to the front door of Santa Rosalita.

He walked to the village hotel euphoniously named the Guest House, registered and went up to a room. He was asleep a few seconds after he had undressed and laid down on the bed.

11

THE PERPLEXING MISS STERLING

DETECTIVE JOHN BRADY, after separating from the newspaperman early in the evening, phoned for a motor car to take him up to the residence. The master of the house and his guests were still at dinner when he arrived and Brady went out on the back terrace, seated himself in a soft cushioned chair, pulled out a cigar and smoked it thoughtfully.

It was the first time he had ever been an unwelcome guest in a house to which he had been brought to solve a crime mystery, and he bitterly resented the situation. He disliked Thomas P. Thompson intensely. If Thompson had made away with his wife, it would give Brady great pleasure to make him pay the penalty for the crime.

It was possible that, since summoning the detective, the millionaire had learned the identity of the killer. Suppose it was his son or daughter-in-law. Or Lida Sterling. As the woman's death could not be concealed, the next best thing had been to remove her from the place where the crime had been committed and put her where an investigator could find no clue to the criminal.

The door of the house opened, and he heard the swish of

a skirt. He looked around and hastened to rise. Miss Lida Sterling had come out on the terrace.

"Do you object to me?" she asked with a fascinating smile. "Please sit down. Mr. Thompson has gone up to his room and the others are playing bridge. You are not the only stepchild in this house. I'm not over popular."

She sank gracefully into a chair opposite him and crossed her fine legs. She held in her right hand a long black enamel cigarette holder. She placed a cigarette in it. Brady sprang up and lighted it. He watched her sharply but admired her in spite of himself.

Miss Sterling was tall and dark and exotic. Her thick black hair was parted in the middle and caught in a thick knot at the nape of her neck. She gazed at him with large long luminous black eyes. She smiled at him enigmatically. He had talked with her the previous day and secured little information. In his pocket was the letter which he had taken from her purse. If she hadn't missed it, he wouldn't be favored with her presence at this moment.

"Miss Sterling," he said. "You were a very close friend of Mrs. Thompson, I understand."

Her eyes met his squarely.

"I was not," she said. "She detested me."

"WHY REMAIN IN a house where the mistress detested you?" he asked brutally.

She lifted her slender shoulders. "Oh, Mona professed to adore me but I knew. And I have no money. I am what one might call a professional guest."

He lifted his eyebrows. "Paid?"

"Board and lodgings," she said frankly. "Disgusting, isn't it?"

"This," said Brady to himself, "is a girl you can talk to." Aloud, "If she hated you, what keeps you here?"

"Because Tom liked me. Mona hated the sight of him and liked me round because he spent a lot of time with me."

"I can't conceive of Thompson having a spiritual side," he said, grinning.

"Tom is unlettered but extremely intelligent. He found my conversation interesting. Mona, being a professional beauty, had no conversational gifts."

"You happen to be a beautiful woman yourself, Miss Sterling. Are you going to marry him, now that he is a widower—?"

"For the fourth time," she finished, laughing. "No, thank you. I shouldn't care for that."

"Not even for financial security?"

"I'll find the right man some day and he won't be a pauper."

"I've heard that you expected to marry him—that you had alienated his affections—"

"No doubt," she said coolly. "Will and his wife are afraid of me. If I married Tom, I should dominate him, which none of his wives ever did. And I might persuade him to leave me his entire fortune. Sometimes I am tempted to do it, just to spite them. An amazingly mean set of young people, don't you think?"

"Rich man's children. Frankly, Miss Sterling, my impression of Thompson is that he couldn't have a tête-à-tête with a young woman who was beautiful without making a pass at her."

"I've never even kissed the man," she said earnestly.

"When Tom and I are alone, which is seldom, he keeps his distance."

"You're a remarkable girl," he assured her. "Who killed Mrs. Thompson?"

"Isn't that your job?" she countered.

He nodded. "I think I'm going to need help."

"Well, Overman is worth investigation. He was in love with her before she met Tom. She induced her husband to bring him out to write his biography."

"But, if he loved her—"

"Men kill the things they love," she said dryly. "According to the poets. So—"

"Between ourselves, have they been carrying on?"

"I never caught them."

She laughed. Her laugh suggested to him the tinkling of Venetian glasses.

"Where are we going, and why?" she inquired.

"Just drifting," he said easily. "Who else hated Mrs. Thompson?"

"I didn't say I hated her."

"You were furious because this writer was making love to her."

She held out her hand. "Kindly return my letter."

Brady laughed. "Not likely."

"It was contemptible to go through my locker."

"A detective must do such things in search of truth. Miss Sterling; I find the situation here astounding. Why did Thompson have the body brought here and try to make me believe that his wife was killed in her bed chamber?"

The woman's composure vanished. Her eyes sparkled, her mouth opened and she leaned toward him eagerly.

"Do you mean to say she wasn't killed in her room?"

"You were at the Nudist Club day before yesterday. You know she was strangled on the roof of the clubhouse."

She clasped her hands together tensely. "I swear I don't know any such thing. Mr. Thompson and I left the others at the Club day before yesterday. We returned about two o'clock. I—I supposed Nona came home later."

HE HAD FIRED his shot and it had missed. Either the woman was telling the truth or she was a magnificent actress.

"Mr. Brady, that letter is of no use to you. Please give it to me."

He shook his head. "My possession of it prevents you from going to Thompson and telling him what I have just told you."

She rose. Her black eyes were smoking with wrath.

"You are a contemptible person," she said angrily. "I wish you good night."

He glanced at his watch. It was nine o'clock. It was vital that he interview the loquacious Miss Smith who had innocently admitted to Duffy the deception which had been practiced.

He went out, crossed the porch and descended the driveway toward the lodge gate a couple of hundred yards below. It was a magnificent semitropic night. There was no moon and the great bright stars cast surprisingly little light. On either side of the driveway the planted terraces extended.

Far below the town glittered and glowed, and the riding lights of the craft moored in the harbor increased the beauty of the spectacle. Half way down Brady had a curious sensation of being stalked. He glanced back and to right and left, but could see nothing, but he was uneasy nevertheless.

He tried to throw off the curious sensation. If ever humans might enjoy happiness and peace here was the place. Yet the inmates of Thompson's Castle were foaming with hatred of one another. Jealousy, strife and death were in that house—and mystery.

He moved on slowly. It seemed to him there was a step directly behind him. He made to turn, a pair of powerful hands grasped his neck and a heavy weight descended upon him.

Brady was a rough and tumble fighter of great experience, a good boxer and a fair wrestler. While only a little above average height and weight, his muscles were like steel and he had extraordinary latent power. But he had been attacked from the rear; his antagonist was tremendously powerful and the advantage was with him. His wind was cut off—he could not make an outcry. He went to the ground, face down, while his enemy straddled his back, jammed Brady's countenance into the pavement and went about the grisly business of choking him to death.

JACK TRIED EVERY trick he knew to dislodge his rider who was naked to the waist. He tore desperately at the hands on his throat. He twisted, writhed, kicked and grew weaker. He could not see his antagonist but he knew it must be the physical instructor, who had attacked Duffy in much the same manner this afternoon, under the impression that Bill was the detective.

He was going—going—in a few seconds he would be gone. And suddenly a pair of headlights appeared at the entrance to the driveway below. A car was coming up.

With an oath, the strangler released the detective's throat, clubbed a huge fist, struck the helpless man a terrific blow on top of the head and sprang away from him, darting into the terrace to the right. A few seconds later the car headlights illuminated a body lying in the middle of the driveway. The car braked. Men shouted excitedly and two persons got out and ran to the body. They lifted the detective and carried him to the car, placed him inside and then climbed in. A minute later they carried him into Thompson's house.

Watkins, the butler, identified him.

"It's Mr. Thompson's detective!" he exclaimed. "Has he met with an accident?"

One of the pair who had discovered the injured man laughed.

"Thought for a minute it was a job for us," he said. "But he's alive, all right. Knocked out."

It was the undertaker and his assistant coming to prepare Mrs. Thompson for burial. They aided the butler and a footman to carry the detective to his room, where he was undressed and put to bed. After that Watkins phoned down for Dr. Olden, the town physician, and went to his employer's room to inform him of what had happened. Finding Thompson lying in bed in a sodden sleep, he decided not to wake him.

Twenty minutes later Brady awoke with a splitting headache and was immediately given an opiate by the physician who was bending over him. The diagnosis was encouraging—contusions of the skull but apparently not a fracture.

12

ACCESSORY AFTER THE FACT

THE WHISTLE IN the morning steamer awakened Bill Duffy, who rolled out of bed and into his clothes. The steamer was bringing the newspapers. One of the greatest pleasures a newspaperman can experience after he has written and sent to press a big story is to get hold of his esteemed contemporary sheets and see how badly he has beaten them. By the time the steamer had made fast, Duffy was on the pier. In a few moments a porter came off carrying huge packages of newspapers, which he turned over to the local news agent. The latter placed them on a truck and rolled them to the magazine and newspaper establishment opposite the head of the pier. Duffy was at his heels.

"Give me all the San Diego papers," he said eagerly.

The packages were open and two newspapers were handed him.

"But I want the *Sphere,*" he said impatiently.

"The *Sphere* didn't come this morning."

"Eh? Why not?"

"I don't know. That's what the steamboat man said."

Bill glanced at the front pages of the rival sheets. There wasn't a line about the murder on Santa Rosalita. His eyes lighted joyfully.

He understood why the *Sphere* hadn't arrived. The first edition had been read by Thompson's agent in San Diego, who had communicated by radio with the island. Thompson had sent word to keep Bill's paper off the island.

Why, the old fool! The old ostrich! He couldn't suppress the news of his wife's murder. What good would it do him?

All the afternoon papers would carry the story; he'd have to prevent all papers from being sold on Santa Rosalita. Thought he was a king, eh? He'd find out.

He went out of the shop. The passengers were coming down the pier one by one. There was a lot of noise at the gangway, shouts, protests.

Bill stopped a passenger.

"What's the trouble back there?" he inquired.

"Why," said the man. "The ship is full of reporters. Seems the *Sphere* carried a wild yarn that Tom Thompson's wife had been murdered. The local police have orders to send the reporters back on the boat."

"But he can't do that."

"Why not? The island is private property. The town is in King Tom's vest pocket. He can refuse to let anybody land he feels like."

Bill whistled and wisely decided to make himself scarce. He had no objections to deporting rival newspapermen. King Tom was sewing this story up for William Duffy. However, some of the local cops might have worked in San Diego; he might be recognized. While the hue and cry was on, he'd be less conspicuous if he were a bather. Bill slipped into the bathing pavilion, thankful that he had left his camera in his room, donned a bathing suit and plunged into the water.

*As he reached for
the railing, he heard
the girls scream*

He swam straight out. He was looking for a small black speed boat. He'd get aboard and loaf there until the steamer departed. Most likely the girl might show up. She had been abroad early yesterday morning. He wanted to have another talk with that girl.

As Bill approached the boat he became aware that it had occupants. He heard female voices. Two girls were lying flat on their backs on the deck. Well, he might as well meet Miss Smith's sister.

He swam around to the stern, leaped and grasped the rail and pulled himself up. As he rose above the railing he heard a slight scream. Two girls sat bolt upright.

Bill was so startled that he almost fell back into the water. One was Gertrude Smith and the other was Iris Dalton, the woman he hated, the woman who had shamefully deceived him.

She recognized him, laughed gayly and waved to him.

"Bill Duffy, as I live," she declared. "Why, isn't this nice!"

Bill clambered on the cabin roof and gazed somberly at the traitress.

"Bill Duffy," he admitted. "I'm surprised you dare speak to me."

"How interesting," drawled the other girl. "Old friends? Why didn't you tell me you knew Mrs. Long?"

"Why, we used to be engaged. I was crazy about him once," declared Iris. "I'm afraid I jilted him. Tom Long was quite irresistible."

"That's why he's an old grouch," remarked Miss Smith. "Disappointed in love. Is he married, Iris?"

"Probably. I wouldn't know."

"Not that it's the business of either of you, but I'm not," stated Bill.

"Furthermore, I'm not ever going to get married. In my opinion women are no good."

The girls exploded with laughter.

"See, you've ruined his faith in women," said Gertrude Smith. "And it's such a pity. I rather liked him, after a fashion."

"You're all the same," he said sourly. "Fickle and untrust-worthy."

"Don't worry, dear," said Iris. "He's only a reporter and I hear he drinks heavily. You haven't lost anything."

"I think he's sort of nice," stated Gertrude with a siren's smile. "And probably you drove him to drink. I thought you were coming to call last night, Mr. Duffy."

"I wouldn't think of it," said Bill untruthfully.

"Oh, I thought perhaps you had come early in the evening. We were dining with Iris."

Bill scowled at Iris.

"I'm not surprised you've turned out to be a nudist," he said nastily. "But this one ought to be ashamed of herself."

"And how do you know I'm a nudist?" demanded Iris hotly.

He grinned at her. "I was peeking through a window in the club house storeroom and I got an eyeful of you."

"Oh," exclaimed Iris. *"Oh."* Her face grew red as fire. She stood up, her slim body draped in a wisp of silk, and then she dived overboard and struck out for the shore with a clean cut overhand stroke.

"YOU'RE A BEAST," said Gertrude Smith severely.

"Good riddance," declared Bill. "That dame ruined my life. Anyway, what's she so touchy about? All the male club members see her parading around up there. Why get fussed up because I got a gander at her?"

"I'd feel the same way about an outsider who didn't understand," said Miss Smith. "I'm glad I wasn't there yesterday. How did you get into that storeroom?"

"I crept through a conduit under the club grounds and there's an outlet into the house. I was coming from there when I passed your house. I'm glad I found you. Detective Brady wants to see you. You'd better tell everything you know. You could be held as an accessory after the fact."

"What do you mean? I had nothing to do with poor Mrs. Thompson's death."

"You don't know the law. Any person who aids and abets criminals—"

"But I didn't," she protested.

"It's criminal to move a body from the scene of a murder and to give out that it occurred elsewhere, because it obstructs justice. Whoever carried Mrs. Thompson from the Club to the Castle is an accessory after the fact. So is a person who knows what was done and keeps quiet."

"But I had to do what Mr. Thompson told me."

"Why?"

"He's my employer."

"He is? What work do you do?"

"I—I'm the ladies masseuse at the Club."

Bill's face relaxed.

"That's different," he exclaimed. "Why pretend you were a member?"

"Well, I didn't see why I should tell you the story of my life."

"You don't parade round with the nudists and play games in your birthday suit?"

She smiled and blushed. "No. I work in the massage room. It's against the rules for employees to use the grounds. Of course all employees inside the Club have to be nude."

"Then what were you doing on the roof?"

"I go up there when the guests have gone and take a sun bath in the late afternoon."

"I guess maybe you're all right," he said cheerfully. "Who was on the roof when you went up?"

"One or two men and several women. They were sleeping. Mrs. Thompson was among them. I went to the end of the roof and lay down and fell asleep. When I woke up only Mrs. Thompson was still there. I went down to my locker and was dressing when Mr. Hopkins told me that Mr. Thompson wanted to see me in the office."

"Was he dressed?"

"Of course."

"Well?"

"He told me that Mrs. Thompson was dead. She was in one of the rest rooms. He said to get her clothes and put them on her. After that, he and Mr. Hopkins and a Mr. Rennick carried her out to a car. Mr. Thompson told me to keep my mouth shut. Next morning he called at my house and said that he was bringing a great detective to the island but in the interest of the Club, it would be given out his wife died at her home. The Club would have to close and I'd lose my job if the facts got out."

"How did you know she was strangled?"

"Mr. Diblee, the physical instructor, told me after the others had gone."

"Did Thompson pay you any money?"

"No. He said he would make it worth my while later."

"Humph. I suppose it's all right for a girl who has to work to take a job like that when she associates only with women."

"But I don't mind being nude inside the Club. You don't understand what a different feeling—"

"Let it pass," he said with a grin. "Gertrude Smith, you're an accessory after the fact. It's lucky you've only talked to me. Brady is under obligations to me and he'll see that you're in the clear."

"But Mr. Thompson—"

"When we get through with Tom Thompson, he won't be able to make trouble for anybody. What do you think of this Diblee?"

"He's a wonderful athlete but rather stupid."

"The women are crazy about him, aren't they?"

"I don't know," she said shortly.

"I've got things to do. Don't tell anybody about talking with me. And don't tell—Good Lord, Iris will yell it all over the island that I'm a newspaperman."

He gazed at the steamer, which was moving out of the port, carrying a dozen disgruntled reporters and camera men.

"In half an hour Brady and I will be at your house. I'll be seeing you."

HE DIVED OVERBOARD. For some reason he was feeling swell. The poor little kid—how he had misjudged her! It was one thing to be a brazen nudist, strolling arm in arm with nudists of the opposite sex; and another to be a paid employee, whose job was massaging members of her own sex. She was a sweet little kid, too. If she liked a fellow— aw, pshaw.

Miss Smith was gazing after him with kindly eyes. In her opinion Wild William Duffy was a person with a certain charm. Iris had been a fool to jilt him, even if he did drink a little. Having met Lieutenant-Commander Long, it was Gertrude's opinion that Iris Long had made a big mistake. The naval officer drank more than a little and tried to make every girl he met. She was aware of that because she had had a passage at arms with Lieutenant-Commander Long in the garden of his house the evening before.

She became aware of a rowboat approaching. She inspected it and recognized Mr. Rennick, who was much about the Nudist Club and who lived down the shore of the island, where he bred goats. With him was a man unknown to her. She waved her hand toward Mr. Rennick and he waved back. The boat was coming alongside.

She gazed in astonishment. Until the night before last she had hardly exchanged a word with the Rennick person. Nevertheless he jumped on board.

"I've something to tell you, Miss Smith," he said. "Come down into the cabin."

"Why—er—"

But he had already gone below. Gertrude followed him down.

"Well?" she said sharply. Rennick laid his hand on her chest and pushed her backwards so that she fell upon a berth. He darted up the steps to the deck, slammed down the hatch cover and bolted it. The other man was getting the gas engine started. Rennick released the mooring line, took the wheel and the boat began to move forward. The girl was thumping her little fists against the hatch cover and screaming but her screams were muffled. In a moment the boat had a bone in her teeth and was moving rapidly toward the gap in the breakwater.

"Lucky that fellow swam ashore," said Rennick to his companion. "We might have had trouble with him."

"I don't like this," said the other man.

"It has to be done," declared Mr. Rennick.

13

BRADY PUTS ONE OVER

DETECTIVE BRADY WOKE from a drugged sleep with a heavy head. Somebody was knocking on his door.

"Come in," he called.

Watkins, the butler, answered.

"Are you all right, sir?" he demanded.

"I guess so."

"Any notion what happened to you, sir?"

Brady grinned. "I've got a faint idea," he said.

"The district attorney and sheriff of Resalva County are in the office with Mr. Thompson, sir. If you're able they would like to have you join them. Do you wish breakfast?"

"I'll see the officers first. Give me fifteen minutes."

He bathed, felt better, went to the office and found Thompson at his desk, shaved, ruddy and apparently normal. Seated in front of the desk like applicants for employment, were the sheriff and district attorney.

"This is John Brady, gentlemen," said Thompson briskly. "Considered the best private detective in the country. This is District Attorney Crane and Sheriff Gibbs."

Jack shook hands and sat down.

Mr. Crane was a plump man of sixty with a small gray mustache, apple cheeks, round brown eyes and little hair.

He was exceedingly well groomed. The sheriff, who was big and raw boned, was chewing gum.

"A very sad business, sir," said Mr. Crane. "A mournful commentary upon our times when a gentleman of great wealth cannot reside on his estate free from the horrible outrages of criminals."

Jack nodded. The fellow was sleek and without force. A speech maker.

"Who done it, Mr. Brady?" inquired the sheriff.

"I have no idea, as yet," said Jack curtly.

"This outrage must not go unpunished, sir," said Mr. Crane earnestly.

Thompson snorted.

"You three talk things over. I can't stand it," he said hoarsely. "Brady, come to my room when you've finished with these gentlemen. Mr. Crane, whether you like it or not, my wife must be buried tomorrow morning."

"As the manner of death is known, I see no objections. Do you, Mr. Brady?"

"Certainly not."

Crane stood up and cleared his throat.

"I wish to say, Mr. Thompson, on behalf of the sheriff and myself that you have our profound sympathy in your bereavement."

"No doubt," Thompson cut in. "Prove it by finding the murderer. Good morning." He strode out of the room.

The D.A., whose speech had died aborning, managed a smile.

"Naturally Mr. Thompson is not himself," he observed. "What is your theory, Mr. Brady?"

"None worth stating at this time."

"Ahem. But we must take steps."

"What do you suggest?"

"Unfortunately, our County has no detective force and the sheriff and his deputies are busy on the main land. I can ask the State Attorney General to send down a special investigator but there might be a day or two of delay."

"Do you want to leave this matter in the hands of the local police?" asked Jack with a smile. This made the sheriff grin.

"Thompson resents County interference," he said. "He told us that you were the best man in your line and we know you by reputation."

"Unfortunately I have no authority here."

"Well, well," said the sheriff. "I'll fix that. I hereby appoint you a deputy."

"You're Thompson's man. You know the ropes here. Why, say, that makes everything hunky dory."

"Give me my commission," suggested Brady.

Obviously both officials hoped fervently that the private detective would do their work for them. Having passed the buck they were elated.

"Thompson told you to keep your hands off, I expect," said Brady, smiling.

"Nobody can tell us what to do," replied Crane pompously. His tone changed. "But we want to be agreeable." Brady could almost hear a check crackling in the breast pocket of the County official.

"By tomorrow or next day I'll have some interesting news for you," he promised.

Gibbs, who was filling out a blank form, handed it to Brady. "Here's your commission. You clean up and give me the prisoner. Mr. Crane will do the rest. I'll get a coroner's jury this afternoon and bring in a verdict of death at the hands of person unknown. We'll make the evening boat back to the main land. Say, it would have been a pretty pickle if this smallpox scare had been the real thing."

"Chicken pox looks quite a little like smallpox at the start," replied Jack Brady. "I'll go up and have a talk with Mr. Thompson now. Glad to have met you gentlemen."

He went out hiding a satirical smile. Thompson's game was obvious. He had persuaded the County to leave the case in the hands of his private detective. When they had gone, he expected to get rid of Brady. Jack had sized up the pair and decided that they could be induced to give him an official position. Now he was a regularly appointed deputy sheriff with authority to accomplish something.

He had put one over on his crafty employer.

HE FOUND THOMPSON sitting at a table on the balcony outside his chamber. There was a highball in his hand and a bottle of Scotch whisky beside his elbow.

He gazed at the detective through half closed eyelids.

"Those fools are going back to the mainland," he said. "They were impressed by your reputation. They expect you to find the murderer. Good riddance to them. We don't need them."

"I'm not sure we don't need the militia," said Brady sternly. "Why are you anxious to prevent the proper authorities from investigating the death of your wife?"

Thompson puffed out his cheeks, his mouth opened and then his teeth clashed together.

"This is too much," he growled. "What do you mean— you—"

"Don't say it," snapped Brady.

"Do you mean I don't want my wife's murderer found?" roared the millionaire.

"That's the way you act," said Brady quietly.

"A paper in San Diego carried the fact that my wife was murdered. I've sent back a shipload of reporters. Have you been talking to newspapermen, Brady?"

"I didn't give out the story."

"You took my boat night before last without my permission. Did you tell the papers what was going on here?"

"I did not."

"Well, it's damn peculiar. Who was the man you dined with last night?"

"Are you having me watched?"

"This is my island. What goes on here is reported to me."

"He was a friend of mine. I dine with whom I please. No doubt the County officers gave out the murder story."

"They claim they didn't."

"Well, it's impossible to conceal it. You're a famous person; your wife was a celebrity and her death a matter of news."

"Then let's have the matter closed up. Find the murderer, Mr. Detective. Didn't you see the fellow who attacked you last night?"

"It was dark and he struck me from behind."

"I wash my hand of you. If anything happens to you, don't blame me. Apparently you can't protect yourself."

Brady's mouth set angrily but he controlled himself.

"Let me ask you a question," he said. "What do you know about Diblee, the physical instructor at the Nudist Club?"

"Diblee? Nothing. He does his work, that's all I know about him."

Brady watched him closely. "Would it interest you any to know that Diblee's real name is Arthur Gomez and that he was your late wife's first husband?"

The shot struck home. The man's cheeks turned purple. His eyes widened, his hands clenched tightly. He sucked in his breath.

"Damn you," he roared. "It's a lie! It can't be true. If you try to smirch my wife's reputation, you dirty, cheap—"

Brady drew the press clipping from his pocket and laid it in front of Thompson. He watched the man closely as he stared at it. He was certain that he had told Thompson something he didn't know and that the news was a bombshell.

"If your wife had been slain at the Nudist Club instead of in her guarded chamber," he said softly, "I would consider this man a very suspicious person."

Thompson was scowling at the clipping. He said nothing.

"Has Diblee or Gomez ever been up here at the house?"

"Certainly not. Absolutely not. He would not be admitted."

"I could make out a strong case against him. He saw his ex-wife living in luxury, happy in your love; in a burst of jealous fury he might have strangled her, assuming he had an opportunity."

Thompson thumped his fist upon the table. "Get him. Send him to the hangman. He killed her. Of course he did. The motive—God knows—probably jealousy, as you say."

Brady was playing him as a cat plays with a mouse.

"Come to think of it, your wife frequented the Nudist Club. She must have seen him. Naturally she would recognize him. If their relations were hostile, she would have complained to you."

Thompson was controlling himself by a tremendous effort.

"I'll be frank with you, Brady," he said slowly. "My wife suggested employing this man. No doubt he was out of work and appealed to her. She was sorry for him."

He spoke softly, but the detective read unbridled fury in the man's eyes. Thompson was positive that Mona's first husband was her murderer, but he was calculating. If Gomez was charged with the crime, it would come out that it had occurred at the Nudist Club. Thompson had some tremendously weighty reason for concealing that fact. Something awful was scheduled to happen to Gomez, but he wouldn't come to his end via the path of justice.

"I'd like to go over to the Nudist Club and have a talk with him," said Brady blandly.

"Keep away from the Nudist Club," shouted Thompson. "The crime took place in this house. One of the guests or one of the servants committed it. You confine your investigation to this establishment."

Brady rose and bowed.

"Very well," he said. "Just as you say, Mr. Thompson. I'd like a car to take me down to the village."

Waiting on the porch for the car, Brady pondered over the determination of the owner of the island to protect the Nudist Club. Its revenue was inconsiderable. Since his wife had met her death there, he should hate the place. He was willing to have the detective suspect his own son and his wife and his two guests rather than risk his learning the truth at the Club.

His game was to let the detective putter around until after the County officers had left and then make things so disagreeable that Brady would drop the case and depart.

14

SOMETHING DROPS
ON MR. DUFFY

AS THE CAR rolled along from the garage, Mrs. William Thompson, the former Jane Jerome, came out of the house. Brady, who had an eye for a good looking woman, got heavily out of his chair as she approached him. Young Mrs. Thompson was wearing a green sports suit which contrasted stunningly with her rich red hair. She smiled cordially at the detective, which surprised him, as hitherto she had been snippy. He wondered whether Miss Sterling had confided to her that the detective had inspected the lockers of the Thompson outfit while they disported themselves at the Nudist Club. If she had learned that Brady had read the letter she carried in her purse, it would explain why she felt compelled to be nice to him.

"I wonder if you'll let me ride down with you, Mr. Brady," she said in her resonant voice. "Watkins tells me you're going down the mountain."

"Sure, Mrs. Thompson. Certainly."

This dame, he thought, had sex appeal plus. Her smile made his blood flow faster. Her greenish blue eyes had the old devil in them. Her full lower lip denoted strong passions; the face was beautiful but hardly what he would call angelic.

Jane Jerome was married to a stick. The bully Thompson had beaten out of his son what character he might have inherited. Of course she had married William for his money and cheated on him whenever she was tempted. The letter he had found in her purse proved that.

"Going to the Nudist Club?" he inquired as he helped her into the car.

"Later. I've some shopping to do. Of course you won't want the car after we've reached the village."

"No, marm. You can have it."

She threw him a warm smile and was silent.

Jack eyed her covertly. Suppose this was the woman who had chased Bill Duffy down the underground passage. Film girls usually have plenty of physical courage and her *dossier* in the *Sphere* office stated that she had begun her career as a horseback rider in Westerns.

"What progress are you making in your investigation?" asked Jane sweetly.

"It's a very perplexing case, Mrs. Thompson," he replied. "Apparently there was no reason why anybody should kill your mother-in-law. There was no robbery. Let me find something to whose interest it was to eliminate her and I'll get a start."

"I don't think you have very far to look," she said significantly.

"Meaning what?"

"There is one person whose interest is obvious."

"Man or woman?" he asked sharply.

She shrugged her lovely shoulders.

"I shall say no more," she retorted.

A moment later the car stopped at the pier head. "Do you wish to get out here?" she inquired.

He descended and she told the chauffeur to go on to the guest house.

"Cat," muttered Brady. "She meant Miss Sterling and nobody else."

Half the persons on the boulevard were in bathing suits and a bather touched his arm.

"Walk along behind me till we get out of the crowd," said Bill Duffy.

Duffy went down upon the beach, which was devoid of bathers at that point, and threw himself on the warm sand. Jack dropped beside him.

"Get any telegrams for me?" he inquired.

"One. It's in my clothes in the bath house. I'll go after it in a few minutes."

"I hear you published the story this morning. Thompson was wild."

"He would have been wilder if I had risked stating that the murder occurred at the Nudist Club."

"What stopped you?"

"I had nothing but Gertrude Smith's statement to that effect, which she might have denied. With Thompson's money and influence, the paper might have got into trouble. Besides we had it exclusively—I mean the fact that there was a murder and I decided to leave something for a follow-up."

"Get your clothes on. I want to see that Smith girl."

"I'll dress and meet you up Canyon Avenue a little ways.

I had a talk with Gertrude this morning. I told her she was an accessory after the fact and she told me considerable."

"I want to hear it from her own lips. Hurry up."

THEY DEPARTED AND Brady strolled a few blocks up the road until he came to a shade tree, where he parked. Presently he spied the newspaperman turn the corner below. Duffy waved his hand cheerfully. When Bill had proceeded half a block the detective observed two men in uniform turn the corner; he recognized by the broad gold bands on his sleeves the chief of police of Santa Rosalita. He was accompanied by a patrolman.

They increased their pace. Obviously they were after Bill Duffy and the newspaperman was unaware of it.

"Bill," called Brady when Duffy was a few paces from him. "You're trailed. Stop as if to ask me a question, slip me the telegram and pass right along. Don't look back."

"O.K.," said Bill out of the side of his mouth. "The local cops?"

"Yep."

"Well, I gave them a run for their money." He stopped, covering the passing of the telegram from the view of those behind him with his broad back.

"What will they do to me?"

"Hold you till the evening boat and deport you."

"Get me out or I'll kick the jail down."

"I'll do my best."

Bill Duffy passed on. A few seconds later Chief Clark, already breathless, drew close and recognized the detective.

"Do you know that fellow is a newspaperman?" demanded the chief. "I have just been tipped off."

"I didn't know it was a crime to be a newspaperman."

"They ain't got any right on this island. I got to pinch him."

"Good luck," said Brady with a grin. Duffy, however, was increasing his lead. Clark cupped his hands. He was a small gray man with a fuzzy mustache and watery blue eyes.

"Hey you, William Duffy," he bellowed. Duffy turned—there was no way of escape, but he made the officers climb another fifty yards to where he stood. A moment later he came down the street between the two officers.

"You've no legal right to nab me, you know," he said as he passed Jack without a sign of recognition.

"We ain't, hey? Young fellow, this island is private property. It's an unincorporated town, owned by Mr. Thompson. When he says newspapermen have to get out they have to get out."

"What are you going to do with me?"

"Send you to the mainland on the evening boat."

Bill laughed. "Then I won't have to buy a ticket. I was going home anyway."

Brady gazed thoughtfully after the officers and their prisoner. It wouldn't do Bill any harm to be quiet for a few hours.

If he tried to secure his friend's release, he would bring the wrath of Thompson on his head. He didn't want to flash his authority as deputy sheriff until the sheriff was safely off the island. Just the same, it was an outrage to lock Bill up.

He opened the telegram. It was from New York. It was signed by the vice-president of the largest banking house in America, a man who knew the inside of everything financial and who was under obligations to Jack Brady. The telegram consisted of about forty words.

Brady read it with eyes which protruded until they almost popped. His heart beat faster and his blood surged through his veins. The telegram informed him that Thompson was not a rich man any longer. He was practically broke.

Chuckling contentedly, Jack thrust the telegram into his breast pocket. So far Bill Duffy had had all the luck, but he had blundered on his discoveries, important as they were and Brady had been blinded by false information from the man who had hired him. Well, Bill was going to lie in the shade of the local jug for a few hours while Jack made hay in the sunlight.

He remembered the house where he and Duffy had failed to find the Smith girl last night and turned in at the entrance. There was a plain young woman sitting on the porch. Brady removed his hat.

"Are you Miss Gertrude Smith?" he asked politely.

"No. I'm her sister."

"Oh. Can you tell me where I can find her?"

The young woman rose.

"No, I can't," she said. "She's supposed to be at the Club at ten. She goes down to the beach every morning early but always stops here before she goes to the Club. I've phoned up there and she isn't there. And her boat isn't at its moorings. I've been down to look."

"Do you think anything has happened to her?"

"Oh, she's a wonderful swimmer. But Mr. Rennick called here about nine o'clock. He said he had a message for her from Mr. Thompson and I'm wondering if he was able to deliver it. Mr. Thompson owns the Club, you know, so it was most important, I'm sure."

"Well, I'm much obliged."

"Do you want to leave your name?"

"Brady is the name. I'll call again. By the way, where does Rennick live?"

"Saltelito. It's a little beach further down the island."

Jack went down the road swiftly and considerably perturbed. The Smith girl was an important witness regarding the place and time of the crime. It looked very much to Brady as if the girl had been carried off to prevent telling what she knew. Apparently she was the only one of those aware where the murder had taken place whose silence could not be depended upon.

Well, he'd get Duffy out pronto, throw a scare into the chief of police and then go into action with his two fisted friend and ally.

CHIEF CLARK WAS seated behind his big desk in shirt sleeves. He was alone in the office, his force of four patrolmen being out on duty. He greeted Brady cordially.

"I hear they going to bury poor Mrs. Thompson tomorrow morning," he said. "I'm certainly glad you made the inspection, Mr. Brady. I—I hate to look at a dead person."

"Have you reported to Mr. Thompson that you arrested this newspaperman, Chief?"

"Why, no. I didn't think it was a good idea to bother him."

"How come you identified him?"

"One of my officers knew him in San Diego and reported seeing him on the beach."

Brady drew from his pocket his commission as deputy sheriff. "Take a glance at that, Chief."

Clark inspected it and returned it.

"I'd take orders from you anyway, seeing that Mr. Thompson brought you here," he said. "When I do call him up about something he bawls me out and says not to bother him. He's a hard man to work for, Mr. Brady."

"Feel like risking your life today, Chief?" asked Brady, smiling broadly. "Do you enjoy a little gunplay?"

Chief Clark turned pale. "Why I—I ain't anxious—"

"That's all right. I think I've located the murderer. He's a tough guy, with five or six killings to his credit. I expect I'll need help. I sized up your cops and I don't think they'll be much good. Bring in this Duffy. He's a friend of mine, a crack shot and he's on the island because I sent for him."

"But why didn't you tell me when I arrested him?" exclaimed the chief, whose relief was obvious.

"I thought it would be a good joke on Bill," declared Brady. "I'm going to swear him into service. Trot him out."

To his satisfaction the chief hopped off his chair and vanished out back. He returned a few moments later followed by Wild William Duffy, who looked a trifle crest-fallen.

"I'm sorry, Mr. Duffy, that I had to lock you up," said Chief Clark effusively. "There is a general order to keep newspapermen off the island."

Bill grinned.

"I was just getting so I liked my cell," he stated. "No hard feelings, Chief."

"How did you work it?" he asked eagerly as soon as they had left the station.

"Told him I needed a man to help me catch a desper-
ate murderer and asked him whether he'd like to let you
go with me or come himself. He elected you without a
second's hesitation."

"Are we going after Diblee, the physical instructor?"

"Not at the moment. I think he'll keep. Ever hear of a
man named Rennick?"

"No, I don't think so. Yes. He was one of those who
carried Mrs. Thompson's body out of the Club night before
last. Gertrude told me that this morning."

"She did? What else did she tell you?"

Bill told him how he had told the girl she was an
accessory after the fact and what the young woman had
informed him after that alarming information.

"Hopkins or Rennick," said Brady. "Hopkins looks to me
like a jail bird. They didn't call in the physical instructor,
who is stronger than both of them, no doubt. Bill, are you
interested in this girl?"

Bill lifted his chin. "Who, me? Say, I'm off women for
life."

"Well, I'm glad you're not in love with her. She has
vanished, Bill."

Duffy grasped his arm tensely.

"Are you kidding? How could she vanish? What for?
That sweet little kid!" he cried excitedly. "What makes you
think so?"

"Aside from Rennick and Hopkins she appears to be
the only person except the murderer who knows that Mrs.
Thompson was killed at the Nudist Club. Rennick called
at her house this morning with an alleged message from
Thompson. Her sister told him she was probably swim-

ming around her boat. The boat is not at its moorings and the girl failed to report for work at the Club at ten o'clock."

"Good God, she may be in danger."

"That's what I think. There is a big game going on here, old man. So big that the death of Thompson's wife is not permitted to interfere with it. You think you saw signal lights from this little coast village when you came in this morning."

"Certainly I saw them. And they were answered at sea."

"Rennick lives at Saltelito, which is the name of the place. I suspect your girl was taken there—"

"Jack, her life may be in danger."

"I doubt it. They want to keep her out of the way until Mrs. Thompson is buried, the County officers have gone and I've thrown up this job and headed for the mainland. I think we should rent ourselves a motor boat and have a look at Saltelito. Got a gun?"

"Certainly not. I don't carry one."

"Well, I've an automatic pistol. Let's go."

They rented a small outboard motor boat and in a few minutes were moving rapidly through the crowded little harbor. Brady was at the wheel.

"What's the program?" demanded the newspaperman.

"We'll look the place over and bring Miss Smith back with us if she's there. I want to meet this Rennick very much. We'll have to adapt our actions to circumstances."

15

TRAPPED

"I APPRECIATE THE way you are coming through for Gertrude," said Bill gratefully. "When you meet her you'll realize that she's a very swell girl."

Jack chuckled. "I don't doubt it. She's going to be a very swell witness. We've got this thing narrowed down, Duffy. As you told the girl, moving the body makes these men accessories after the fact. Thompson, too, for that matter."

"Do you eliminate Thompson as the murderer?"

"Well, I'm inclined to. It's curious. The fact that a pillow was used to strangle her makes me think that a woman might have done it."

"Why?"

"Well, a brute like Gomez wouldn't care, but a murderously inclined woman would be more apt to cover up the victim's face. We know Gomez didn't use a pillow on you and me."

"How do you know a pillow was used?"

"Because there were no marks of any sort on the throat. My throat is black and blue. I put on a high collar to hide the discolorations."

"Can't you make this thing go faster?" pleaded Bill.

Brady grinned. "But you don't like women. You don't care about this girl."

"I'd go to the rescue of any woman in danger," declared Duffy.

"But you wouldn't be in such a gol-danged hurry. There's Saltelito up ahead."

They had been skimming along close to the shore but avoiding the breakers which beat against the base of the high cliffs. A mile or so ahead the beach of Saltelito was visible.

"Doesn't look like much of a place," commented Duffy.

"No. Bill, it would certainly have been a great help if you had got a look at the naked dame who chased you down that conduit."

"Why bring that up?" asked Duffy resentfully.

"Because a woman with nerve enough for that would have nerve enough to strangle Mrs. Thompson. She thought you were me—that's why she opened fire on you."

"Yeh. She had an exaggerated idea of your perspicacity," said Bill sullenly.

The boat headed on for the little settlement. The place was very small, four or five bungalows widely separated, and a decayed looking boat landing.

"Do you see Miss Smith's motor boat?" demanded Brady.

"No. It's not here. Probably she isn't here at all. They took her somewhere else."

"They've concealed her boat perhaps. Anyway, we'll know soon."

As he spoke a man came out of a cottage; lifting a pair of binoculars, he inspected the approaching craft.

Brady headed for the landing where two small boats

were tied up and the man on the beach began to make gestures to keep off.

"Not very friendly," commented Duffy. He did not alter his course. He saw the man go into the nearest and largest house. Then his keen eye discerned a telephone line, which left the house at the rooftree and ran fifty yards to a rock which stuck up like a long finger, after which the line was not visible.

While it was most unlikely that Thompson's telephone company would run a line this distance to serve a single patron, there was, nevertheless telephone connection between Saltelito and Santa Rosalita Village.

The boat bumped against the landing.

"I'm going ashore alone," Brady told the newspaperman. "In case of trouble I'll fire a shot and you cast off and make for the port."

"Like hell I will."

"You're unarmed, you idiot. Don't you see, they won't dare to put me out of business when you're at large? I can handle this. I don't expect any opposition."

Without waiting for an answer he leaped ashore.

THERE WAS NO sign of life in the settlement as Jack walked toward the largest of the bungalows, a white painted wooden affair of the type one buys in a department store and which can be erected in a few hours.

His right hand sought his jacket pocket and closed lovingly around the grip of his automatic pistol. He knew there were people here who didn't wish visitors and he had a fair notion of their character. He knocked at the door with his left hand. A young man opened it, a good looking young man whom Brady had never seen before.

"I beg your pardon," the detective said. "I thought this little settlement looked picturesque and I took the liberty of landing. I wonder if I could get a drink of water."

The young man flung the door wide open.

"Certainly, sir," he said heartily. "Won't you come in?"

Jack was covertly inspecting the interior. It was a room fifteen feet square, skimpily furnished and in great disorder. There were no other occupants.

He stepped into the room, his hand still clutching the weapon in his pocket, but less tightly. There was a slight sound behind him. He whirled and gazed into the muzzle of a heavy Navy revolver.

"How are you, Brady?" inquired its owner. "I'm wondering if you remember me. It's a long time since we met."

An old trick, which Jack had used himself more than once, and he had fallen a victim to it. When the door had been flung open, it had concealed the second occupant of the room. He had known he might be walking into a trap; he should have expected something like this.

"Snappy Sam Coleman," he said coolly. "I thought I had planted you in Atlanta for ten years."

"Frisk him, Ollie," commanded Coleman. "Take your hand out of that pocket, Jack, if you please."

Jack released his weapon reluctantly and dropped his right arm at his side. One did not argue with Snappy Sam when he had the drop on one. It was a beautiful afternoon. There was no more peaceful spot on earth than this little settlement. Nobody could possibly look less dangerous than Snappy Sam Coleman. But Brady knew that he was in deadly peril; that his prospects of escaping from this trap alive were one to a hundred.

Coleman was a dapper little man. He had the sort of face that men forget. He was the perfect type of average man. About five feet six in height, weighing about a hundred forty-five pounds, wearing rimless spectacles upon a small nose. He had mouse colored hair, was clean shaven and mild mannered. And he was as vicious as a copperhead and crafty as the father of all serpents.

"You hadn't ought to butt in on my graft, Jack," he said reproachfully. "That sort of thing can't be squared."

"You've got me wrong, Sam," Jack said aggrievedly. "I've been out of the Secret Service for years. Booze and dope runners don't interest me a little bit. I'm on this island to find out who killed Mrs. Thompson and I know you didn't do it."

"Tie this bird to a chair, Ollie. He's slippery as an eel and foolish like a fox."

A few minutes later Brady, bound so tightly with a swordfish line that he could move only fingers and toes, was seated opposite Snappy Sam. Sam was wearing white flannel trousers with a very wide stripe and a purple coat. One noticed Sam's clothes when he put on the dog and did not notice his features; to escape identity, all he had to do was to change his clothes. If he had a weakness, it was that he was garrulous. Jack's only chance was to play on that.

"Jack," Sam said. "Four years in quod is a long time. A fellow has time to think what he'll do to the guy who put him there, when he gets out."

"Get any interesting ideas?" inquired Jack blandly.

"Several. I've been on this graft, which is the best thing I ever got hold of, while you were in the East. Business

before pleasure, you understand. I was going after you
sooner or later, though."

16

DEAD MEN SAY NOTHING

"AREN'T YOU UNREASONABLE, Sam? My job was to get you. Yours was to avoid me. You can't blame me because you fell down on your job."

"You made love to my girl. That's how you caught me."

"That's wrong," protested Jack Brady. "I never made love to a moll for the sake of catching her man."

"You're a blasted liar," cried Sam loudly.

Brady shrugged.

"I sent some wires to Washington from San Diego, Sam," he said significantly.

"The replies won't do you any good. Ollie," he called, "come outside with me a minute."

The youth who had admitted Brady went out of the cottage with the criminal. Sam returned alone almost immediately. He grinned at his prisoner. Suddenly he stopped and listened.

A shot had been fired and the surrounding cliffs echoed and re-echoed it.

"I sent Ollie to get your boatman.

I reckon he got him," stated Coleman.

Brady cursed himself for bringing Bill Duffy unarmed

with him, but the eyes of his tormenter were gazing eagerly for evidence of distress.

"Think of everything, don't you?" Jack said very softly.

"Yeh. I'm trying to think of a swell way to send you to hell."

Jack managed a laugh.

"Let's discuss something else," he suggested. "You and Thompson must have made a barrel of money out of the dope racket."

"What do you mean, Thompson?" cried Coleman sharply.

"Don't kid papa," said Brady, grinning. His only chance was to keep the fellow in conversation. Maybe Duffy had got away. Bill was resourceful. Why hadn't Ollie returned?

"This is my game. Thompson's a multimillionaire."

"The Chief of the Secret Service told me recently that the country was being swamped with dope, though the regular channels had been plugged up. Tom Thompson's been broke for a couple of years, which is why he went into dope smuggling with you, Sam."

"You're crazy," shouted Coleman.

"I'm running this alone."

"You're on salary. Thompson must be making three or four hundred thousand a year out of the racket. What do you get, ten per cent?"

"I don't have to argue with you," said Sam ominously.

Brady laughed sneeringly. "Thompson owns the island. He controls the County officers and has the customs inspectors under his thumb. If he wasn't in on it he could run you out of here in a day."

"Would he have brought you here if he was running a racket?"

Brady laughed. "I think he acted impulsively without consulting a fellow named Coleman. Naturally he was upset. His beautiful wife had been murdered. Any notion who killed her and why, Sam?"

Sam scowled at him. "I got to think of something new in deaths. Something lingering. Like the Chinese. Sawing a man in two, eh? Or staking him out and let the ants eat him. Only we haven't got those kind of ants on this island."

Despite his stout heart, Brady turned pale and Sam saw it and gloated.

"Blow off the top of my head and be done with it!" pleaded Jack. And he was half serious. Without assistance he could not escape from the heavy fish line which bound him. And Snappy Sam, like a great many dope runners, used the stuff himself. Full of hop he was capable of torturing a victim.

BACK IN THE old days when Brady had been chasing Coleman, the dope merchant, he had got on his trail through a girl whom Sam loved and whom he had shamefully abused while crazy with cocaine. Jack hadn't had to make love to her. She was thirsting for revenge.

"Take your time, take your time," advised Sam. "You'll keep. I'm getting to be a rich man, Jack, no thanks to you. Boy, this is a racket!"

"How do you work it?"

"I don't mind telling you. An invention of mine. They drop the stuff overboard from the China boats, attached to a life buoy. This has a time arrangement on it and starts to burn an electric light five minutes after hitting the water.

It goes over close to a reef north of here and we have no trouble picking it up. You know how much we can pack in a suitcase?"

"About forty thousand dollars worth."

"Right. And everybody that leaves on the excursion boards has a suitcase or a hand bag."

"You ought to be in a mood to forget and forgive."

"Oh, yeh?" His grin was significant.

"You were the boy with the women," remarked Jack. "I suppose you've fixed yourself up on this island."

"And how!" exclaimed Snappy Sam. "Class, Brady, class. If you were going to be round any length of time I'd give you a knockdown to this one."

"Nudist, isn't she?"

"Eh? Well, sure. So am I. Why not? Everybody's doing it."

"Look here, Sam. I'm after the Castle murderer. I'll make a deal with you."

Sam lifted both hands and dropped them palms down.

"You make no deal with me, feller," he declared. "You ain't safe to have around; besides, I hate your guts. I'm leaving you now to see what's happened to Ollie. Enjoy yourself."

He left the bungalow, slamming the door hard behind him. It was characteristic of Brady that he devoted his solitude to fitting into its place what he had learned from Coleman instead of fretting about a demise which seemed unavoidable.

It was some satisfaction to have arrived at a correct conclusion with nothing to go on. To get as much line as he could on Thompson, he had wired his banker friend in

New York for a confidential report on the financial status of King Tom. The reply handed him by Bill Duffy stated that the rumor was correct, that Thomas Thompson's corporate fortune had been swept away by the Insull debacle but that he seemed to have large private resources.

Brady knew that before a captain of industry quits he throws his private fortune into the breach. Thompson must have been broke, owning nothing but the island. He must have been easy to convert to the notion of using it as a base for dope smuggling on a large scale.

How he had come into contact with Snappy Sam Coleman, the dope expert, didn't matter. Sam was running the executive end of the concern.

Brady knew now who the male nudist was who had been conversing with the woman when Bill Duffy listened in at the Nudist Club. Not the physical instructor but Sam Coleman. Had Coleman sent the giant up to Thompson's to murder Brady? It seemed probable. Coleman was Rennick, the goat man.

Jack thought he understood, now, why Thompson had given out that his wife had perished in her chamber on the mountain top. The Nudist Club was the headquarters of the dope ring.

17

"WORDS ARE GOLDEN"

UNABLE TO MOVE hand or foot, aware that his end was probably near at hand, Jack Brady fumed because he was so near a solution of the island mystery and his death would make his discoveries useless.

Snappy Sam fancied himself as a lady-killer and had a certain success. A woman had been with him discussing the presence of Brady on the island. This woman was even more eager to get rid of Brady than Coleman, since she had led the pursuit of the eavesdropper down the conduit beneath the Nudist Club. Coleman naively boasted that his present sweetie had class. Jack reverted to his original idea that a woman was more apt to use a pillow to suffocate a victim than a man.

Coleman's girl friend might have murdered Mrs. Thompson. That would explain her anxiety to dispose of the detective.

Was she one of the young women at the Castle? They would represent Coleman's idea of class. Both had been at the Nudist Club yesterday morning. A motion picture Western star, and a self-confessed adventuress. Spurious ladies. Either of them capable of an affair with the enterprising Snappy Sam Coleman.

His eyes roamed desperately around the room. He might tip over his chair and crawl about, but there was no object visible which would be helpful toward getting rid of the fish line which was cutting into wrists and ankles. And time was passing. Maybe Duffy had escaped.

Sam Coleman had to kill him. Even if he hadn't been nursing a hate against Jack Brady for years, he had to kill Brady for his own safety and that of Thompson. The door was opening. Could Duffy—

No. Coleman and Ollie entered. Sam was scowling and Ollie looked much perturbed. Ollie. Where had he heard that name before? There was a certain slight resemblance—

Coleman rushed into the inner room. Ollie looked distressed.

In a few seconds Coleman came forth with a rifle. He turned an evil grin on Brady.

"Going to give you time to repent," he sneered. "About an hour, maybe. Ollie, you stick here till I come back. Don't take your eyes off that snake for a minute."

He went out, slamming the door. Ollie sat down in a corner, picked up a magazine and turned the pages listlessly. Jack stared at him and a certain conviction grew slowly upon him.

"How does it feel to be a murderer?" he demanded.

The young man scowled.

"I didn't kill him," he said. "I couldn't shoot a man down in cold blood. I ordered him out of the boat. He shoved off and started his motor. I drew bead on him. Oh, I'd have shot him if he had pulled a gun. I fired a shot over his head. He kept going. I let him go, damn him."

"So Sam has gone after him. He won't catch an outboard motor in a rowboat."

Ollie said gloomily, "We've a fast motor boat concealed up the beach. He'll get him all right."

"So you didn't break completely with your father," Brady said smiling.

"What in hell do you mean?" shouted the youth. He was clean cut, a bit dissipated looking but not vicious. Brady would not have been captured so easily if this youth had awakened his suspicion when he opened the cottage door.

"Your name's Oliver Thompson, young fellow. Working for your father, eh?"

"Damn you," the youth shouted. "It's as Sam said. You know too much."

"Ollie, if you don't release me, your father will be hung for the murder of his wife," Brady said loudly.

Ollie closed his fist and struck Brady in the mouth so hard that the chair went over backwards. From the floor Jack smiled up at him.

"I can save him. Nobody else can," he said with an assurance which carried conviction.

Young Thompson stooped and lifted the chair and Brady to a sitting posture.

"There's nothing in it for you to have your father die. You're making more this way than you'll inherit," said the bound man.

"Suppose you say what you have to say," Thompson said in a voice which was unsteady. "Who thinks my father killed his wife?"

"The managing editor of the San Diego *Sphere*, Mr.

The door flew open and a burly man rushed in

William Duffy. He was at the Nudist Club today and made a discovery."

"Wha—what's the evidence against father?"

"Do you know who Diblee, the physical instructor at the Nudist Club, really is?"

"Joe Diblee. He used to be a wrestler."

"He is Arthur Gomez, who was your stepmother's first husband. Does that suggest anything to you?"

Thompson felt for a chair and dropped into it.

"Yes," he said in a low tone. "Mona persuaded father to hire him."

"It will be alleged that your father discovered his identity. That he had reason to believe that the child she was going to have was not his. And under the influence of a drug he strangled her with a pillow."

"That's your case against him. You can't prove it."

"Young man, thousands of persons have been convicted of murder on circumstantial evidence less persuasive than that. I admit it was my case. Duffy knows what I had discovered. But today I have learned something which indicates that your father is innocent. I now believe that Mrs. Thompson was killed by a jealous woman. I have a threat against her life in this woman's handwriting."

"Then that's all right," said Thompson with a sigh of relief.

Jack shook his head. "Unfortunately I have confided this to no one. If Sam Coleman murders me, Oliver, he practically condemns your father to the gallows."

"THIS IS A gag to get me to let you go. It won't work," cried Ollie furiously.

"Sam Coleman wants to kill me in revenge for a business which doesn't concern you in any degree. My presence on this island is known. I have powerful friends in high places. There will be an investigation by the Federal government beyond your father's power to stop, assuming he isn't in jail waiting trial for the murder of his wife, and your profitable drug traffic will be uncovered and those connected with it punished. An hour ago I told William Duffy I was coming here."

"He said you could make black sound like white," muttered Thompson.

"You shouldn't let a hophead's lust for revenge send your father to the hangman," said Jack earnestly.

Thompson began to pace the room.

"I've urged my father to quit this game," he said excitedly. "I've never trusted Sam. He's savage as hell." I'm not on the island very much. I'm supposed to be in wrong with Dad. He likes me better than he does any of the others."

"Cut these ropes and be quick about it," said Jack persuasively. "And you've got to find a way to get me to the village before Sam gets back."

"Are you going to expose this racket?"

"I'm going to arrest the murderer of your stepmother. That's my business here."

Thompson whipped out a knife, stepped behind Brady, who for a moment winced lest the knife be buried in his back. But the youth severed the cords which bound him, and Brady was free. He had talked himself out of the worst mess he had ever been in. In the past he had been rescued from death traps and fought his way out. Never before had he worked a spell with words. But, never before had he had to deal with this kind of criminal.

"You're a sensible young man," said Brady, wriggling his fingers and toes to restore circulation. "This jig is up. Washington is going to swoop down here in a day or two. For your sake I'll try to keep your father out of the mess and by night I'll have the murderer of your stepmother under lock and key. Now where's Miss Smith?"

"You mean the masseuse at the Nudist Club?"

"Yes. Where did he hide her?"

Young Thompson looked bewildered. "Why should Sam hide her anywhere?"

"Because she knows your stepmother was killed at the Club, not at her home as was given out. She has disappeared."

"I only arrived here a half hour before you turned up. I know nothing about Miss Smith."

"We'll look around," said Brady grimly.

"Better hurry," said the young man nervously. "Sam went after your boatman in a speed boat. He may be back at any minute."

Brady grinned. They hadn't searched him, hadn't even removed his automatic from his hip. He had been captured and roped, and Sam's original intention was to put a quick end to him.

"Glad to see him," he remarked.

Search of the other cabins revealed nothing, but in the abandoned goat pens up back he saw two mules, saddled and bridled.

"What's the idea?" he demanded.

"There's a rough trail out of here across the high mesa which comes out above the Nudist Club. It's about fifteen miles. We'd better take those mules and go that way. I don't fancy explaining to Sam how you got away."

"Huh. Much used?"

"Only when the sea is too rough for small boats."

"Well, I've never ridden a mule, but I'll try anything. Let's go."

18

THE MOUNTAIN TRAIL

AS THEY RODE up the canyon behind the goat pens Brady observed that the trail was well defined and he thought he understood why it was used. He glanced whimsically at the pale, worried youth who rode beside him.

Brady had had to lie for his life. The best thing which could have happened to King Tom would have been to have Brady disappear off the map; instead he had persuaded Thompson's son that it was the worst thing.

"What are you going to say to Sam when you do meet him?" he inquired.

"I'm hoping to make the steamer for the mainland without encountering either him or father," replied Oliver sullenly.

"I suggest you go to Los Angeles and lie low till Sam is back in prison."

"I have your word that my father won't be accused of killing Mona?"

"Unless something happens to me, he won't."

"Will you explain to him why I had to scram?"

Brady nodded. "You're too decent a kid to be a criminal. Where has Sam cached his dope?"

"I'm saying nothing about that."

"You know his girl friend, don't you?"

"I never saw her."

"But you know who she is."

"No."

"I'll tell you. She's the woman who murdered your step-mother." He eyed Thompson obliquely.

"I hope you can prove it," said Thompson dourly. Jack was disappointed; he had hoped his startling statement would cause an outburst which might be illuminating.

"I'm going after the evidence now. Which of the women at your father's house is Coleman's sweetie?"

"Look here, if you don't know, how do you know who killed Mona?" demanded Thompson angrily.

"Duffy, the newspaperman has seen her with him, but I haven't. I need to tie her up with Coleman."

"All I know is he meets some woman at the Nudist Club. I don't know if she is living at the Castle. Say, maybe it's Miss Sterling."

"Look here. You've seen her with him at the Club."

"I'm lying low. I haven't been there for a year."

"Your father will marry Miss Sterling, won't he?"

"I don't know. I hope not. He's in no position to marry anyone if this racket busts up."

Having decided regretfully that Thompson could not help him along this line, Jack dropped the subject. They had climbed a long distance while they talked and were almost on top of the presumably inaccessible mesa.

"Happen to know the terms of your father's will?" he asked.

Oliver laughed bitterly. "He can't get over the notion he's still a multimillionaire. The island has been in the red for a couple of years and the income from the racket just about keeps up his establishment. William, the good boy, will have to scratch for a living."

"Don't your brother and his wife know that your father has lost his fortune?"

"You bet they don't."

"What's that house over there?" demanded Brady, pointing away over to the left.

"It's a shack for goatherds. Dad had a notion that he could people these hills with goats, but they couldn't get enough to eat. It's abandoned now."

"I see."

Brady's mind was busy with what he had learned and what he proposed to do about it. When the trail forked and that on the left pointed toward the distant shack, he hesitated. There seemed no sense in investigating the place. He wanted to get back to Santa Rosalita. So he took the right hand fork, complacently oblivious to the fact that Gertrude Smith was a prisoner in the shack.

He tried not to think about Bill Duffy, whose prospects of escape from the man with the rifle in a speed boat were slight. If Bill had been slain Coleman would hang instead of going to prison for twenty years.

After another half hour the trail broadened. Here the harbor could be seen. It looked as though adventurous horseback riders came up to this point more than occasionally. A few minutes more and he could see the Nudist paradise, a patch of dark green with an oval of blue water, an oasis in the surrounding desert. He kicked his mule and the two men increased their pace. Coleman should be back at Saltelito by this time, Jack supposed. He grinned to think of his fury at the escape of his victim and was pleased that he and Thompson had taken Coleman's only means of transportation across the top of the high cliffs.

19

ADVENTURES OF BILL DUFFY

WILLIAM DUFFY SQUATTED in the little motor boat and watched his friend go up to the nearest house and knock on the door. He saw the door open and Brady enter and then the door closed. He waited several minutes with increasing anxiety. Brady had told him to go back to the Village if a shot was fired, but Duffy wasn't built that way. However, things were quiet. Maybe Brady was mistaken in thinking this place was dangerous. Maybe Gertrude hadn't been kidnaped at all.

By and by a man came out of the house and headed towards the boat-landing. He gestured to Bill to come ashore. This didn't look right. Brady would have summoned him himself.

The fellow was coming up rapidly. He stuck his hand in his pocket. Bill started the motor and prepared to cast off the line. The man had pulled a gun. He was at the landing.

"Come out of there and come up to the house," shouted the gunman.

Bill shoved off and grabbed the wheel, presenting his back to the weapon. The boat darted away from the landing.

"Come back here or I'll shoot."

Bill dropped into the bottom of the boat, giving her all the gas she would take and holding onto the wheel.

"Bang."

A bullet whizzed over his head. Brady had walked into a trap. Bill couldn't go back and enter the trap too. He had to get to the police at Santa Rosalita. Let him shoot.

But no more shots were fired. Bill looked back. The man on the landing lifted the gun threateningly. Duffy thumbed his nose at him. He was almost out of revolver range.

He was tearing along the shore line. Now he was beyond the beach and had to swing quickly to port to avoid a frowning cliff against which the breakers burst with a savage roar.

He was not an expert at driving an outboard motor boat, but he knew how to steer and he had to make time. The coast of the island was jagged and irregular; its limestone cliffs rising to great heights. There was an offshore breeze and seas were rolling in and smashing viciously against the cliffs. Bill kept just outside the breaker line— he had no time to swing out to sea where the water was smoother. In a couple of minutes he was out of sight of the little cove of Saltelito but, because of the contours of the shore, the village of Santa Rosalita was invisible. He was driving right into the blinding sun. The little flat-bottomed boat bounced up and down and the motor roared savagely. He was getting a lot of speed out of the thing. Not enough, though. They might murder Brady. He began to cut corners.

Suddenly the high cliffs loomed over him and cut off the sun. If he had had a gun he would have gone after Brady; he would have shot it out with the fellow on the landing.

He swung round a jutting promontory and gave a gasp of dismay. Directly ahead was a solid wall of rock. He was crossing a rocky inlet in which the water was boiling. He whirled to port. Too late. A big sea caught the frail craft broadside and swamped it. It turned over. And Bill Duffy was struggling in foaming seas.

He was dragged under. He fought his way to the surface. He was rolled over and over like a ball.

A big rock brushed his shoulder. He swallowed a whole sea, so it seemed, but he fought on. He was washed on a table of rock; then, before he could gain a foothold he was swept by another wave to the opposite side. But now the table rock broke the force of the seas. The waves were less overpowering here; only fifty feet distant was a gap in the cliffs. A fellow could get a foothold if he could cross the short stretch of swirling water. He had to try. The waves were carrying him in. He bumped against boulders, miraculously escaping anything worse than bruises; after what seemed an eternity he crawled out of the water upon the rocks.

"WOOF," EJACULATED BILL Duffy. He lay flat trying to get his wind back. Feeling better after a couple of minutes, he sat up, He was just in time to see a speed boat passing well out. He shouted but the breakers drowned the shout. And then the boat was past. It looked to him very much like Gertrude's black motor boat. She wasn't in it. There was a man at the wheel and nobody else visible.

As there was no other settlement, the boat must be coming from Saltelito, which meant that Gertrude was there. And he was caught in this cleft in the cliffs. No, it wasn't a cleft, it was a sort of canyon. He discerned a faint trail. Glory be, there was a way out of here to Saltelito.

No chance whatever of getting to Santa Rosalita without a boat. He'd go back and see what the element of surprise and a pair of fists could do about Jack Brady, the boob, and Gertrude Smith, the darling.

He rested another five minutes and then began to climb up the canyon. The trail was almost impossible. It might be all right for goats but not for humans. It went up. Always up. It twisted and turned. In no time all his muscles ached. Duffy had been leading a sedentary life lately.

An hour passed and he was still climbing. At times he crossed ledges which were six inches wide, clinging to jutting rocks with his fingers. He began to wonder if it went anywhere. There seemed no doubt that it would land him to the top of the cliffs, if he didn't fall off and break his neck.

He rounded a bend and to his horror there was a goat on the narrow ridge just in front of him. The goat gazed at him reflectively.

"Hey, scat!" commanded Bill Duffy. The thing's eyes gleamed evilly, like red lights. It lowered its head and it had formidable horns. And then it charged.

The goats on the island had not bred very well and the attempt to create a herd had been abandoned while the survivors went wild. This goat was wilder than Wild William Duffy. Bill gripped a sharp finger of rock at his right with both hands. The path was hardly eighteen inches wide. He lifted his right foot defensively.

Crash. The living battering ram struck Duffy's right boot, and as it did Duffy kicked out toward the left. The shock of the collision almost jarred his grip loose and seemed to have driven his thighbone into his abdomen. But the outward pressure was fatal to his antagonist. It was William goat instead of William Duffy which went off the ledge and went rolling and crashing down the side of the precipice, uttering a weird cry.

"Gosh," gasped Duffy. "I hope there aren't any more. I'm not up to meeting another one."

At the end of half an hour, the trail ascended less abruptly and he emerged in a depression upon a high mesa. And at the bottom of the depression there was a hut.

"There must have been a goatherd living up here at one time or another," remarked Duffy. "Nobody else would live in a place like this." He was at an elevation of at least fifteen hundred feet and the view from the spot where he stood was sublime. Bill however was in no mood to contemplate the beauty of nature. He moved rapidly toward the hut. He was dog tired and in the hut there might be a cot. Its door faced the other way; after a moment of hesitation he hastened around the corner of the structure, which was not more than twelve or fifteen feet square and constructed of rough stones picked up in the vicinity.

Rounding the corner he stopped short in astonishment. A man was squatting on the stone doorstep.

"Hello," cried Bill cordially. "How the heck do I get down to Saltelito from here?"

The man was a large, crude, unshaven person who needed a haircut. He had small black eyes and his complexion was Mexican. He was as much astonished as Duffy himself, but his reaction was different. He drew from a belt a long sheath knife and with a snarl sprang at the weary mountain climber.

THIS WAS TOO much. With a bellow of rage Bill Duffy met the rush. He ducked under the upward sweep of the knife and caught the slasher's wrist with his left hand. He drove his right straight into the fellow's nose. The man cursed him in Mexican and pulled his knife free. Duffy kicked him swiftly in the groin, which caused him to groan and double up. Duffy caught the knife wrist again, This time with both hands, while the left hand of his antagonist grasped the unprotected throat. And then a woman screamed loudly, as the door of the hut opened and a second man appeared with a heavy cane. He swung it, brought it down upon the head of the fighting Irishman and that was all that was necessary to finish temporarily a fellow who had had a hard forenoon. Bill went down and out.

He had a curious feeling a few minutes later, as though his face was wet. He lifted a feeble hand to wipe off drops of water. He opened his eyes. There was Gertrude Smith. Her face was within six inches of his and her tears were dripping on his face.

When Bill opened his eyes Gertrude Smith exclaimed, "Bill, darling," and she put her soft lips against his and wet his face with her tears some more.

"I—I didn't dare hope you would come, but I prayed you would," she sobbed.

"Heroic newspaperman rescues kidnaped beauty," he muttered. And under his breath he added, "By accident."

"Excuse me," she said stiffly. "Of course you only hunted for me because it would make a story for your damn paper." She sat up and away from him. Bill sat up.

They were inside the hut. By the light from a small window he saw that Gertrude was in her bathing suit, just as he had left her on the boat. Her face was dirty and her eyes were red from weeping, but she was a very remarkable looking girl withal and apparently she was fond of him. While their acquaintance was sketchy and he certainly hadn't given any reason for her to believe he would risk his life searching for her, Bill thought he would let her continue to think so. Those kisses had been pretty sweet.

And come to think of it, he had been hunting for her. He and Jack Brady, poor devil.

20

THE AFFAIR AT THE HUT

"THEY HAVEN'T HARMED you, have they?" he demanded belligerently.

She shook her head. "I'm all right. I've only had some goat's milk to drink. It's very nasty. Did they hurt you very badly?"

He grinned. "I was doing all right until eight or ten more of them hopped on me."

"You were wonderful. There are only two of them, but one had a knife and the other hit you with a big stick."

"Where are they now?" he demanded.

"Outside the door in the sun."

"Why did they carry you off?"

"I know too much, so I heard Mr. Rennick say."

"Then Brady was right."

"You mean the detective? How did he know I had been kidnaped in my own boat?"

"He put two and two together. He wanted to have a talk with you. Good Lord, poor Jack Brady is in their hands. Can you get to Saltelito from here?"

"Yes. They landed me there and these two men took me up here. Isn't that the way you came?"

He grinned. "I chose the worst way."

"But how did you know where I was?"

"Lady, I didn't. I sort of stumbled on you. I thought you were at Saltelito."

"Have you been in the water? Your clothes are sort of damp."

"In, under and over it. I had a fight with a goat back on the trail."

"Oh, oh," she wailed, "he's delirious from the blow on the head."

"Look here," said Bill, "I didn't start after you for a story. Nobody ever heard of you and your kidnaping wouldn't even get on the third page."

"Then why did you come?"

He blushed. "Because I kind of liked you—now, don't you get any idea I'm in love with you. I've had experience with women. They're good to look at but they ain't sincere. I found that out."

"Huh. You go risking your life for girls you only kind of like," she commented scornfully.

"That's what you call chivalry. Men have to do that," he smiled. "I will say that you are a very beautiful girl and good company—more like a fellow than a girl."

"I understand," said Gertrude. "You feel like a brother to me. You're afraid because I kissed you that you'll have to marry me. Why, I've heard about you from Iris. I wouldn't marry you on a bet. You're a drinking person and rather worthless."

"Yeh? Then why did you kiss me?" he demanded angrily.

"You goof, I'd have kissed a wooden Indian. I was scared to death, afraid of night coming on with those two awful goatherds. I'd have welcomed anybody."

"Oh," said Bill, convinced. "I see."

"It isn't as if you had done anything," she continued with hauteur. "You came upon this place by accident. You haven't accomplished a heroic rescue. You're a prisoner, just like myself. You let two low persons beat you up. And you look like a scarecrow."

"Swell," said Bill with his fetching grin. "Now that we understand each other, let's be pals. You tell me what happened to you and I'll tell you of my adventures. As for the rescue, I'll do that, too, not because I have any especial regard for you but because my good friend is a prisoner at Saltelito and I have to get down there and turn him loose."

"Hadn't you better go alone? Won't I be a bother to you?" she asked acidly.

Her eyes met his; they scowled at each other for a second and suddenly both smiled understandingly.

"You're all right," said Bill. "I expect you're the girl who is different from all the others. How are you?"

"I'm fine. But if I'd turned you over to the police yesterday morning for evading the quarantine, I suppose I'd be massaging plump ladies at the Club at this minute, instead of being confined in a nasty hut with you."

"I think this is quite nice," stated Mr. Duffy. "And if you had a clean face and hands you'd be marvelous."

"It's a pity you can't see yourself," she retorted. "Why is your friend a prisoner at Saltelito? Why was I taken there and then brought up here?"

"Brady has it doped out that Saltelito is a smuggler's base and that Rennick is head smuggler. There is some connection between these fellows and the murder of Mrs. Thompson. I don't know just what.

"Brady is a mysterious duck and is always afraid I'll publish something before he is ready. If he had been frank with me, he wouldn't be in the pickle he's in now. Though I couldn't do much, not having a gun."

"I never heard of smuggling on the island."

"Well, it's going on all right. I saw signals exchanged between Saltelito and a ship at sea last night. What kind of a bird is this man who slugged me. Another Mex?"

"No. He's an American. A surly brute. He was in here with me for hours and I couldn't get a word out of him."

"You're lucky, I'm thinking."

She smiled a little.

"He didn't seem interested in me," she said. "The Mexican laid a hand on me and he made him go outside."

"Then he isn't a bad sort. It's too bad I've got to slug him."

THEY WERE SITTING side by side on the floor. She grasped his right arm with both hands.

"Don't be a fool," she pleaded. "We're in no danger. He has a gun and the other man a knife. Don't start anything."

There was a wild gleam in the newspaperman's eyes.

"It's not that I don't enjoy your company, Gertie," he assured her, "but Brady is certainly in danger of his life. Several attempts have already been made to kill him. I've got to take a hand."

"No, no, you'll be shot."

But Duffy was on his feet. He moved over toward the door. It opened inward. He stepped to the right of the door frame.

"When I lift my hand," he said softly, "open your pretty

mouth and scream blue murder. They ought to have tied me up. Very careless of them."

"I won't," she said. "You can't make me."

"Listen, kid. I have a chance to jump them if you scream. If you don't, I swear I'll pull open this door and rush 'em. Now!"

He lifted his hand. She saw that he was in deadly earnest. She opened her mouth. From it came a high pitched screech to curdle the blood. It sounded as though a woman was being hacked to pieces by knives.

He heard a shout outside. The door flew open and a burly man rushed in, a revolver in his hand. Bill rose on the ball of his left foot, swung his whole body behind it, and struck the man a terrific blow on the left temple. He went down like a chopped tree.

The second man, who was at his heels, drew back, his teeth bared in a savage snarl.

"Come here, you," cried Duffy, who had grasped the gun from the floor, where it had fallen when its owner went out.

The Mexican stepped back a dozen feet. Bill menaced him with the revolver.

He saw the flash of the knife in the fellow's hand, saw the arm drawn back and pulled the trigger. The bullet was faster than the knife. It struck the Mexican in the chest a hundredth of a second before the weapon darted from his hand.

Cling. The knife struck the door frame and dropped to the ground; the Mexican went over sidewise and lay still. Bill turned pale. He hadn't intended to do more than wound the man in the knife arm, but he aimed so badly that the bullet entered the torso. He bent over him. He was dead. Bill rose slowly in great distress and Gertrude screamed again—this time not in feigned terror.

The other thug had got upon his feet, grasped her and stood in the doorway, holding her in front of him as a shield.

"Drop that gun, you—" he roared, "or I'll choke the life out of her."

He shifted his left hand to her throat. The girl's eyes were dilated with fear, her mouth was open piteously.

Bill almost dropped the weapon—the death of the Mexican had unnerved him—but he instantly rallied.

"I'm a dead shot," he lied. "Your legs are exposed, mister. Set the lady down. Take your hand from her throat. Say, I can pot you in a dozen places."

The man glared at him and then weakened. He set Miss Smith on her feet. She instantly darted to her companion's side. The arms of the kidnaper were above his head.

"Smart fellow," said Bill approvingly. "Now step inside. Remember I've the gun, so don't come after us."

"You've killed Ramon," growled the man. "You'll swing for it."

"Oh, I don't think so. But, having killed one, I'd just as soon kill both of you."

Without a word the man stepped inside the hut.

"Come on, kid," commanded Bill. "Show me the way to Saltelito."

Miss Smith took his arm.

"Going to be hard on your tootsies, isn't it?" he asked solicitously.

"I'm used to going barefoot. Bill, did you have to kill that man?"

"I aimed at his hand. That's the kind of dead shot I am," he said ruefully. "But his knife would have killed me if it had hit me. I'm sorry, dear."

"You are rather wonderful," she said softly. "We go in this direction."

21

BRADY GOES NUDIST AGAIN

WINDING DOWN THE mountain side, they lost sight of the Nudist Club for awhile. Ollie Thompson was deep in mournful thought and Brady had plenty to think about, so they had ceased to speak. After a time Ollie drew rein.

"We leave the mules here and they find their way home," he said. "Just around the bend we enter a ravine which runs below the Nudist Club. It's a comparative short walk down the ravine until it comes to a road. Brady, I'm glad things have worked out as they have."

Jack shook his hand gratefully.

"A thing like this, aside from the moral aspect of supplying addicts with dope, is damn rotten," he said. "You're lucky to be out of it, boy."

They passed through a very narrow rock passage, talking, and suddenly they were in a gulch beneath the wall of the Nudist Club. Jack recognized the place from Bill Duffy's description and sought the entrance to the conduit. He spied it but not in time to see a man dart through the hole, a man who had been trudging up the canyon and had heard approaching voices.

Jack and Oliver continued along the ravine until it crossed the paved road and there Brady stopped.

"Good luck," he said. "I'm going to pay a call at the Nudist Club." He glanced at his watch. It was getting on to mid-afternoon. The trip across the mesa had taken fully two and a half hours. He walked thoughtfully up to the Club entrance and rang the bell.

"Tell Mr. Hopkins that Mr. Brady is here," he requested of the attendant.

"Yes, sir. Please step inside, sir."

In the reception room the manager met him, deeply concerned.

"What do you require this time, sir?" he demanded.

Brady laughed. "I'm here as a guest. I have a notion that the rays of the sun will be very beneficial to me."

Hopkins' pale face cleared and he smiled, much relieved.

"Certainly, Mr. Brady. This way. I'll open a locker for you."

Jack peeled off his garments swiftly. Hopkins regarded him dubiously.

"You're not tanned, sir," he said. "You want to be careful. You could get a bad sunburn."

"I'll try to keep in the shade."

"The light is very strong. Would you like dark glasses?"

"An excellent idea."

"And hadn't you better cream your nose and upper lip?"

Jack's eyes sparkled. "Let me have all the fixings. A shower first."

When Brady came out of the shower, Hopkins set to work to cover his nose with a thick coating of cold cream and carried the covering over his upper lip. After that he produced black goggles. Jack put them on and inspected himself in a mirror.

"Marvelous, so far," he exclaimed. "Now let's see what I can do about it."

BRADY HAD BROWN hair but the hair on his body was black. He drew from his right hip pocket a small flat package which he opened and shook forth a black wig. While the manager stared at him astounded, Jack fitted the wig over his hair. Taking the cold cream he proceeded to cover his forehead in such a way as to make it difficult to discern that he was wearing a wig.

When the job was done he was certain anyone would have difficulty in recognizing him; it was most unlikely that any of the group from the Castle would guess his identity.

"How many people are here, Hopkins?" he inquired.

"About thirty for lunch, sir."

"Are they still at lunch?"

"Most of them are back on the grounds."

"Many of them covered up like myself?"

"A number, sir."

"Good. I should be sorry to learn that you tipped anybody off as to my identity."

"I know on which side my bread is buttered, Mr. Brady."

"O.K. Let's go. What's the routine?"

"All members and guests may speak to one another without an introduction. The principal rule is that no person may make any comment of any sort whatever regarding the personal appearance of another."

"I'll remember that," said Jack, smiling. "Let's go."

Hopkins opened the door which admitted to the Club proper and John Brady walked through it with apparent sang-froid. Despite the previous visit, he had never been so uncomfortable and self-conscious in his life. He knew that he was blushing beneath his coat of cold cream. He was for the first time dismayed because he had knobby knees.

However, there was nobody in the huge sun parlor which he had entered, and in the dining room beyond he saw a man and woman lunching in a far corner who were as undraped as himself and totally oblivious of their nakedness. He turned right and found himself in a hallway with a staircase mounting to a second story. There was a sign at the head of the stairs. "The Roof."

Jack went up to the roof, a bare expanse, upon which a dozen canvas cots were set out, only two of which were occupied.

He became aware of eyes staring at him, female eyes. He turned sidewise and leaned against the parapet. He heard a snicker. Cautiously he inspected the pair of sun bathers. They were young women who were not members of the Castle party. They were laughing at his self-consciousness, confound them.

From the parapet he had a good view of the grounds. There were two or three people disporting themselves in the pond. He saw several stretched on the grass at its edge, shaded by a huge palm tree; and over at the right, he saw that an archery contest was going on. A man was shooting at a target and a dozen people were sitting or lying in the vicinity watching the course of the arrows.

Aside from the nakedness of everybody, a Sunday school picnic might have been taking place. And Jack, who was not a Puritan, was forced to admit that it was a pretty spectacle. A sheet of shining blue water; a park of dark green; flowers, trees, thick turf; and brown, graceful male and female figures, as unconcerned as people must have been in the groves of Diana of Ephesus.

Great artists had painted pictures of this sort of thing, pictures of the Golden Age. He thought of the gardens of Aphrodite at Alexandria, of the Eleusinian mystic rites, of the figures on Greek vases.

Though he couldn't identify people he was close enough to observe that all the women below were slender and graceful. Fat women would never go in for Nudism. There were one or two men below who suggested Bacchus rather than Apollo. Men who had the delusion that women didn't care how the male sex looked.

The man who was shooting at the target was Diblee or Gomez. He handed the bow and quiver of arrows to a young woman with flowing black hair, a young woman who was as slim as a boy, as graceful as a dryad. It was Lida Sterling.

22

FLIGHT OF AN ARROW

FULLY HALF THE people in the grounds had dark glasses and whitened noses. He would attract no attention if he went down and mingled with them. But Jack was stricken with overwhelming shyness.

Lida Sterling drove an arrow which stuck in the outer rim of the target. She shot another arrow and missed completely. There was a burst of laughter.

It broke the charm of the spectacle for Brady. Below were a lot of people with no more morals than rabbits, no more principles than cats. There might be nudists who were fanatic sun-worshippers, but not the party from Thompson's Castle. These were ultrasophisticated and decadent people. Among them, perhaps, was the killer of Mona Thompson.

And one of the women, he suspected, was carrying on a love affair in this phony Arcadia with one of the most vicious criminals in America. The place was headquarters for other illicit affairs, no doubt. Moderns, he thought, cannot throw off the conventions of two thousand years with impunity. This Nudist Club had bred wickedness and it had bred murder.

He mustered his courage and walked down the steps.

This time he did not turn his back to the young women who were watching him from the cots, and he was not disturbed by the ironic laughter which followed his departure.

He pushed open the door and walked toward the archery court. He passed a long, slim young man lying on his stomach who glanced at him curiously. It was Overman; obviously he had failed to recognize the detective.

Jack approached several people who were squatting on their haunches at the right of the archers. They paid him not the slightest attention. He threw himself on his stomach on the turf and buried his face in his arms, his ears alert for stray remarks. All comments, however, were regarding archery.

He confidently expected Coleman, alias Rennick, to appear presently. Coleman, alarmed at the escape of his prisoner, would hasten to the place, which Jack knew now to be headquarters of the dope runners.

Criminals never had had a more remarkable and secure base. Because it was a private club and a resort of nudists, access to it by investigators was impossible. On this island, owned and ruled by Thompson, whose police were Thompson's paid employees, they had the advantage of sanctuary here. It was not only a sanctuary, it was a citadel.

When Bill had described the drainage system elaborately, Brady had thought it curious; but at the time he was far from being convinced that Thompson's island was a smugglers' base. Now he was certain that the conduits beneath the Club were a storage place for opium.

Coleman, naturally, had been terrified when Thompson had brought Brady, his ancient Nemesis, to the island.

Learning of it, he had warned Thompson of the peril to their business from the ex-Secret Service ace. That explained the attempt to make Brady believe that the murder had taken place at the residence. He must be kept away from the Nudist Club at all costs.

Coleman, who had boasted of his racket to the man he intended to kill, would have warned Thompson of their mutual danger from the recent escape of John Brady. His life wouldn't be worth a penny on this island unless he struck first. Yet he had risked wandering out into the Club grounds, nude and unprotected, because Coleman would come here and consult with his woman.

Let him identify the woman and Jack thought he would learn the identity of the murderer of Mona Thompson. If this woman was "class" as Coleman boasted, she would not be a partner in the dope racket; and her fear of Detective Brady, her anxiety to kill him, which had sent her down into the conduit ahead of Coleman, was due to something else. She was afraid he would pin Mona Thompson's murder on her. And if she had killed Mona Thompson, it was certain that she was one of the three women at Thompson's Castle.

SOME MINUTES PASSED and he heard a plop as a body dropped beside him. He lifted his head. Lida Sterling was sitting close to him.

"So curiosity overcame you, Mr. Brady," she said softly and mockingly.

He sat up.

"I'm afraid you are too clever for your own good," he retorted. "How did you recognize me?"

"Oh, your disguise is perfect. I happened to be on the

A man and woman were seated at the bedside
of a form covered with a sheet

roof awhile back and saw you walking up the road. Do you expect to find a clue here, or are you taking time off from your job?"

"I thought a sun bath might make my think tank function better," he said with a grin.

She smiled back at him. "It seemed to me to be rather sluggish."

"Is it proper for a male and female nudist to go strolling?" he inquired.

Lida laughed wickedly. "So long as they keep walking. As a matter of fact, we do exactly as we please. Let's stroll toward the pond."

He dropped back as they moved away together and he heard a musical chuckle.

"What are you laughing at?" he demanded.

"You're blushing like a child," she replied. "Nudity is nothing, Mr. Brady. Make a note of that."

"Nudity as practised here," he retorted, "is a form of viciousness and you know it."

"I am afraid we were all vicious before we paid our first visit to this club," she said with a half sigh. "Shall we swim?"

"Don't you think Rennick might resent that?"

"Rennick? Oh, yes. The goat man. He doesn't interest me, Mr. Brady."

"Mrs. Thompson said that he did," he replied.

She glanced at him obliquely. "Crude work. I don't prattle, Mr. Brady."

Jack glanced around. The sun was burning him, and there was a high thick hedge close to the pool which cast a pleasant shade.

"Shall we sit down?" he inquired.

"Why not?" she asked gayly and flung herself on the turf. He seated himself near her, not too close.

"Miss Sterling," he said slowly. "I've been thinking about that letter. Let me see your hands. Strong hands, strong wrists. You hated Mona because Overman liked her. You love Overman but you would marry Thompson if Mona left him free. I think you found Owen making love to Mona. Wild with jealousy, you choked her to death under a pillow or a towel."

She thrust her dark beautiful face close to his. Her eyes blazed. "You lie and you know it."

At the moment Jack was quite unconscious that he and this beautiful young savage were sitting, almost touching, in a state of nudity.

"The police would consider it a strong motive," he

replied. "You hated Mrs. Thompson. You had the opportunity—"

"You know I didn't do it."

"But I think you know who did. You are in deep water,
Miss Sterling."

Twang. Swish.

Something darted past the left arm of Jack Brady. Something warm and red splashed against his breast. The shaft of
a two foot arrow stuck out of the bosom of the girl beside
him, who moaned and fell back on the grass.

23

THE MURDER ARCHER

BRADY SPRANG LIKE a tiger for a clump of bushes fifty feet away. Scratched and bleeding he emerged on the other side. He stood upright. He stared in all directions. There was a group in front of the target and a man was drawing a bow. He saw a man lying on his stomach fifty feet to the right. He rushed to him and grabbed him roughly by the shoulder. It was somebody unknown to him.

"What the devil do you want?" the fellow demanded angrily.

"Did you see anybody running?"

"No, why?"

"A woman has been hit with an arrow, shot from those bushes."

"The devil you say." He leaped to his feet. "Where?"

"Right there. Is there a doctor here?"

"I don't know. I'm a guest. I don't know anybody."

Brady rushed to the archery group.

"Miss Sterling has been struck by an arrow. Is there a doctor among you?" he shouted.

There were screams. Shouts. People ran round in circles. Jack saw Overman running at top speed in the direction to which the man he had first roused was pointing.

"Get Diblee," screamed Jane Thompson. "He knows what to do." The physical instructor was visible coming from the exit of the clubhouse. Brady gazed searchingly around. He saw Jane and William Thompson in the mob running towards the scene of the shooting.

Brady remained alone at the archers' stand. The target was at right angles to the spot where he and Lida had been reclining. By no possibility could one of the persons shooting at a mark have sent an arrow in that direction. And it would be spent before it reached its object. Besides, he had heard the twang of the bowstring and the arrow had seemed to come from that thicket.

Diblee was running like a deer toward the spot where Lida lay. Jack saw him elbow his way through the naked throng. A moment later he emerged, carrying the wounded girl in his arms as though she were a feather. Overman was by his side and the others streamed after them.

Horribly puzzled, Brady walked back to the spot, seated himself as he had been sitting when the tragedy occurred. He had been facing the thicket. The girl had leaned toward him in her anger and indignation; he had turned sidewise and then—the arrow. It certainly had been fired from the bushes.

He walked over to the thicket and examined it carefully. It was about thirty feet in length and about six feet in depth.

Getting down on hands and knees, he explored the thicket at several spots. Finally he went around to the rear.

Who had shot the arrow? Overman and the Thompsons were accounted for. Gomez or Diblee had been in the house. His eyes fell casually upon a bit of uprooted sod. He stared. There was a circle of sod two feet in diameter, in the center a round hole about an inch and a half in diameter. Was it the manhole cover described by Bill Duffy?

WITH AN EJACULATION of excitement, Jack dropped on hands and knees and tried to lift it. Impossible. He muttered angrily. Then he saw, lying against the edge of the thicket, an iron bar about eighteen inches long. With a grunt of satisfaction he crawled to it, returned and jammed its curved end into the hole. It gripped. He tugged and lifted the manhole cover, which had been ingeniously camouflaged with sod. Without the slightest hesitation he lowered himself into the hole, taking the iron lever with him. He failed to touch bottom, dropped and landed about ten feet below the surface.

By the daylight which penetrated through the hole he found himself in a tunnel, over six feet in height and two and a half feet wide. There were water pipes on either side.

It was, in truth, the tunnel described by Bill Duffy, the scene of his battle with the naked woman.

"Ah!" cried Brady triumphantly. "So this is how it was done."

The arrow had been aimed at his breast. He had turned as it left the bow, and it had driven into the bosom of the unfortunate girl beside him.

And the arrow had been shot by the physical instructor. Hopkins had informed Gomez of the identity of the new arrival. Gomez, who had failed to kill the detective by strangling him, had tried the efficacy of an arrow.

He had lifted the manhole cover, let go his arrow, dropped into the hole and pulled the cover back into place, but not quite. He had fled through the tunnel to the house, and had appeared at the clubhouse door when the alarm was given. A perfect alibi. And as Lida was a person against whom he had no grudge, he would do all in his power to save her life.

Well, Brady had learned enough to throw the brute into jail for attempted murder. Dropping the bar, he set forth along the tunnel.

24

THE BATTLE OF MOLES

BRADY WAS IN the arm of the tunnel which was designed to drain the pond. Ahead somewhere was a side tunnel which led into that storeroom Duffy had described. He would reach the house, go to the locker room, get his revolver and take Gomez down to the jail with him.

Presently he saw light ahead and was able to move more rapidly. In a few minutes he found himself looking out into the gulch through which Duffy had fled to safety. Somehow, he had passed the junction with the other tunnel.

As he turned he made a discovery which had escaped the newspaperman. There was a groove in the floor of the tunnel; and above was a runway upon which a door was housed. A peculiar door, fashioned from a series of narrow steel plates. It was a watertight door which, when pulled down, hermetically sealed the tunnel. Brady whistled softly.

This was the most elaborate drainage system with which he had ever come into contact. Much too pretentious for a little institution like the Nudist Club.

He began to retrace his steps carefully. This time he wouldn't miss the side opening.

He came at last to the fork in the passage and he turned to the right. He had proceeded only a short distance, however, when a sixth sense told him that there was some-body else in the passage. It was total darkness, eyes could not become accustomed to it. He stopped and listened intently. He could hear the pad of naked feet. He could hear breathing. What to do? He was unarmed. He had laid down the iron bar near the manhole.

Run for it.

He turned and ran. The thing behind him ran, too. It was gaining. Gaining rapidly. Apparently, it could see in the dark. Blind as a bat, Brady was overhauled before he had traveled twenty yards. He had to make a fight for it. He turned, crouching in the narrow, black passage, and the unseen enemy was upon him. It dove at him head first, knocked his feet from under him, but as the black bulk plunged, Jack dived over it.

He knew his opponent now. Gomez, the football player and wrestler—thirty pounds heavier, three inches taller; a professional against an amateur. Men in their pelt. Prim-itive men. The battle would be to the death—Jack Brady's death.

But he had pulled his legs into the air and Gomez had struck them with his head, not his arms, and had failed to grasp them. Brady was up ahead of the other fellow and away. Back along the passage, arms touching the walls, feet flying. If he could reach the exit into the storeroom—not a chance! Gomez was bounding along behind him, gain-ing again.

Jack dropped to hands and knees. Crash! Gomez had collided with him, and toppled over him. Something hit the concrete floor with a sickening thud. He hoped it was the brute's head. Jack stepped on the man's back, leaped beyond him and continued his flight. Fool! He should have run the other way, toward the exit to the Gulch. Too late.

It seemed that Gomez had knocked himself out, for there was no pursuit for a couple of seconds. No, he was up and coming again. Where was the right hand opening? With a gasp of dismay, he realized he must have passed it. **BRADY, OF COURSE,** was anything but a coward. He could wrestle and box and win nine rough and tumble fights out of ten. Gomez was his master but he would not have hesitated to fight him in the open. Here, in a two foot passage, there was no chance to side-step, circle or evade a wrestler's charge; with those two great hands upon him, there would be only one outcome to a clinch.

No word had been spoken in this battle of moles. No bargain was possible, no compromise.

Ahead there was a ray of light—the manhole cover was ajar. Was there a ladder to the surface? There must be. Only, Gomez would be on him and tear him from the ladder; not a chance in the world. And Gomez was coming up fast now. Not twenty or thirty feet behind.

Jack's flying left foot encountered something hard and heavy and a yelp of pain escaped him. He had broken his toe against a movable object. With an ejaculation of delight, he stooped, groped and came up with the lever which had moved the manhole cover in his hand.

He turned and Gomez catapulted into him. Wham!

The iron bar came down. It missed the head but struck the left shoulder. With a howl like an animal, Gomez's right hand closed on Jack's right shoulder and felt its way to his throat, while the left endeavored to secure the weapon. Jack brought up his right knee and caught the wrestler in the groin. The man's left hand almost touched the lever, missed and collided stunningly with the right side of Brady's head. Like a bull Gomez jammed his head against Jack's chin. And, the head being thus located, Brady, half choked, half knocked out by the butt, with an expiring effort, brought the bar down upon the skull of the wrestler.

It was enough. The grasp of Gomez relaxed, he dropped to the floor of the tunnel, and Jack went out on his body. Something revived him almost instantly. Something cool and wet. Water was swirling along the bottom of the tunnel. The death grapple had taken place in an inch or two of swiftly running water without either of the combatants being aware of it.

Brady, staggering to his feet, stared stupidly into the dark. He heard a swishing sound, like water escaping through an open faucet, an enormous faucet. And the water was rising rapidly. It was up to his ankles.

Somebody had turned the valve which emptied the huge pool into the conduit. Jack stooped. Gomez's face was under water. He grasped the inert mass by the shoulders and lifted it. Already there was a swift current pulling at the calves of his legs. In a few moments the tunnel would be filled with a roaring torrent. He and Gomez would be swept along by an irresistible force, their heads battered against the roof, their lungs filled with water. Drowned like rats in a trap. Deliberate murder by a person who wished both Brady and Gomez out of the way.

If he could get up through the manhole. The passage in which he stood continued on and under the pool. The manhole cover was at least five feet above his head. He reached up. There was a round opening in the roof of the tunnel which led upward to the exit. There was a ladder. With one arm around the big torso of the wrestler, he stretched upward. His fingers touched the lowest rung of the iron ladder on the side of the manhole shaft. He had dropped down without noticing it. He might pull himself up, but he would have to abandon Gomez, whose head had been cracked by the blow of the iron bar. He couldn't abandon him. He was a brute but human. Besides, Jack needed him in his business.

THE WATER WAS rising. It was up to his thighs, and its pull was terrific. Jack grasped the rung of the ladder with his right hand and hugged Gomez with his left. The water continued to rise and the current to increase in strength. It swept his feet from under him. He managed to brace them against the side of the tunnel. The strain on his arm was painful. He set his teeth. Steadily the water climbed higher. Jack managed to get Gomez across his thighs, held him with a death grip. Minutes went by. Through a great pipe, the water was pouring out of the pool, but now the current, somehow, was not so strong.

This puzzled him for a minute and then he understood. The water-tight door at the gulch exit had been closed. It was intended that the conduit should be filled completely, so that there should be no possible escape for the pair, trapped below ground. The water was now three feet deep. In a few minutes it was four feet. And Jack Brady smiled.

The closing of the lower door, which was intended to drown Gomez and himself, was going to save them. He never could get up that ladder with the two hundred twenty pound wrestler in his arms. But, unable to escape into the gulch, the water would rise into the shaft and lift them to the surface level. All he had to do was to hold on for a few minutes longer.

It was more than a few minutes, however, before the water reached the tunnel roof and forced the bodies of the two men up into the shaft. Brady would have been compelled to let go his hold except that as the water rose, the weight he carried was partly supported by it. The current had rapidly decreased in strength. He was able to reach the second and then the third rung of the ladder then, grasping Gomez by the hair, he held his head above water with little difficulty. It became evident, when his own head was within twelve or fourteen inches of the manhole cover, that the water would rise no higher. There was no longer a suction. Getting his feet upon the bottom rung and holding on with a monkey's grip, he pushed against the cover with the top of his head and lifted it clear of the opening.

A nude man was only thirty feet away and walking in his direction. It was Owen Overman.

"Overman, help," he shouted. "Help. Quick."

The novelist looked around, stared to right and left, and finally sighted the human head sticking out of the ground.

"By God, it's Brady!" he exclaimed. "What the devil are you doing in that hole?"

Jack had his shoulders braced against the edge, his feet on the ladder and both hands fastened in the wrestler's hair, holding head and chest above the surface of the water.

"Quick. I can't hold out," he pleaded.

Overman was at the edge of the shaft.

"Get hold of him," gasped Brady, laboriously.

The writer dropped upon his stomach, peered down into the hole and saw what the detective was holding.

"Let me get a grip on him," he exclaimed. "Move a bit. Now. Is he dead?"

"Not yet. Hold him till I get out."

He crawled out and fell exhausted on the sod.

"I can't lift him," cried Overman.

Jack rallied. "Can you hold him till I get a rope?"

"Sure."

Staggering to his feet, Brady trotted feebly toward the clubhouse. He observed that most of the nudists were at the brink of the pond, watching the shrinkage of its waters.

His strength came back rapidly and he was almost himself again when he rushed into the building. There was nobody in sight but there was a push button on the living room wall. Jack pushed.

Immediately Hopkins appeared from the locker room. At the sight of Brady he turned deadly pale and looked as though he had seen a ghost.

"A rope, quick. A rope, damn you," shouted Brady.

Hopkins vanished into the men's locker room and returned with a coil of rope.

Jack snatched it from his hands and rushed out of the building. When he arrived at the manhole, however, he found his aid was not needed. Overman's shouts had brought several men to the rescue; the huge, naked body of Arthur Gomez, alias Diblee, lay on the grass.

"LOOKS LIKE A fractured skull," Overman remarked as Brady joined him. "Dr. Olden is attending Lida. Some of you get him."

"How is Miss Sterling?" asked Jack anxiously.

"A nasty wound, but not fatal," the novelist replied. "Fortunately it was not a barbed arrow. If I can find out who discharged it, by God, I'll murder him."

Jack nodded towards the unconscious physical instructor.

"You can have him when I'm through with him," he said. "He shot that arrow. He intended it for me."

He grasped Overman's arm. With a furious imprecation, Overman had been about to throw himself upon the body on the grass.

"Save him for the hangman," said Jack softly. "You're mad about Lida. Why don't you marry her?"

"I would if she'd have me."

Jack laughed and patted him on the naked back. "She will, I feel quite sure. A lot of strange things are about to happen. Come with me."

Brady led the way back to the clubhouse. He pushed open the door of the men's locker room. There was an attendant there wearing white duck trousers but naked to the waist.

"Open my locker, please," said Brady.

"And mine," said Overman. "I've had enough of this."

Jack dressed rapidly, felt of his pocket and the automatic lying therein.

"Where's Mr. Hopkins?" he demanded.

"In his office, sir."

Brady was not one to cling to a theory in the face of facts. At one time he had suspected Gomez of killing his ex-wife; he had switched to the notion that it was a woman's job when he learned of the naked woman who had pursued and attempted to shoot Duffy in the conduit.

Gomez's various attempts on the detective's life, he had assumed, were inspired by the smuggling gang of which he probably was a member. In that case, why had the contents of the swimming pool been turned into the tunnel when Coleman, who must have been lurking about, had learned that the detective and Gomez had gone down there?

It would indicate that Gomez was not in Coleman's gang, that the physical instructor's murderous assaults on himself were motivated by something else.

Why did Gomez wish to kill the detective? And why did another person want Gomez eliminated? He could solve the mystery if he had time, but he had no time.

He opened the door of the locker room which led into the reception room. At the left of the reception room was a door marked *office*. He opened the door.

25

THE WEAK LINK

MR. HOPKINS WAS at his desk speaking into the phone when Jack Brady burst into the room. Brady slammed the door; placing his back against it, he covered the manager with his pistol.

Astonished and startled at the apparition of a man apparently in murderous rage, Hopkins pushed back his chair and dragged himself to his feet.

"What—what's the meaning of this?" he gasped.

"Don't you know?" thundered the detective.

"Am—am I under arrest?"

"You're not going to be arrested," shouted Brady. "You're going to be filled with lead, you crawling, murderous cockroach. Why did you turn the water into the conduit, eh?"

"I didn't. I swear I didn't do it, Mr. Brady. For God's sake, don't shoot."

"I'm going to count three and let you have it."

Whimpering like a dog, the man dropped to his knees and stretched out his arms imploringly.

"Don't shoot me. I'll tell all I know."

Brady concealed a smile. He had anticipated that Hopkins could be thrown into a panic.

"Who turned on the water if you didn't?" he demanded.

"It was Mr. Rennick."

"You mean Snappy Sam Coleman. Where is he?"

"He left a few minutes ago." Hopkins had crawled around the desk and was still crouching. Brady deliberately kicked him.

"Get up, rat," he commanded contemptuously. "I'll give you a break if you tell the truth."

"I swear—"

"First, where's the cache of dope?"

"In a watertight room below the conduit, sir. Near the manhole you went into."

"Who's Coleman's woman?"

"I—I don't know, sir."

Brady scowled. "No use fooling with you." He lifted his weapon.

"It's Mrs. Thompson, sir, the one who was Jane Jerome."

Brady sucked in his breath. He had evidence that Jane was in the habit of cheating on her husband.

"Was Gomez one of your mob?" he demanded.

"No, Mr. Brady. He's too dumb to be any use."

"I see. You, Coleman, and Oliver Thompson ran the dope business."

Hopkins nodded. "And you and Coleman carried the body of Mona Thompson up to the Castle the other night."

"Yes, sir."

"Where did you do time—Leavenworth?"

The man swallowed hard.

"Atlanta, sir," he confessed.

"When did Coleman get here?"

"About an hour ago."

"And you told him I was on the grounds. Answer me."

"Yes, sir. I had to."

"Get away from that desk. Stand against the wall."

The club manager obeyed. Brady patted his pocket but he was unarmed. Seating himself at the desk, Jack picked up the phone with his left hand, covering the prisoner with the revolver in his right hand.

"Give me the Castle," he told the operator. "Castle? Watkins, please, and hurry it."

When the butler came on the line he asked eagerly, "Is the Sheriff still there?"

"Holding an inquest, sir."

"Get him to the phone."

"Sheriff," he exclaimed when that official arrived at the telephone, "get a car. Pick up Chief Clark and a couple of his officers and come immediately to the Nudist Club. It's Brady. Yes. Big doings."

He hung up.

"You'll find out you can't get away with this stuff on this island," asserted Hopkins.

"I'd really prefer to shoot you, you rat," said the detective vindictively. "Just say another word."

HOPKINS RELAPSED INTO affrighted silence. Brady kept an eye on him while he tried to fit Jane Jerome, the film star, now Mrs. William Thompson, into the picture. Jane Thompson was the nudist who had pursued Duffy down the conduit with a gun. Jane was the girl friend of Sam Coleman. The situation was so tangled as to be bewildering. Gomez had gone into the conduit to kill Brady, Sam Coleman's enemy, and Coleman had turned on the water to drown both Brady and Gomez. What was the physical instructor's animus against Brady? He was not a smuggler and not the murderer of his ex-wife!

Upon the failure of his plot, Coleman had fled. Had he gone back to Saltelito? Would he escape from the island or continue the battle? Brady was torn between a desire to pursue the dope smuggler and give the works to Jane Jerome Thompson. While he was still debating there was a knock on the door.

"Who is it?" he demanded.

"The police are inside and insist upon being admitted, Mr. Brady," called a servant.

"Let them in."

A moment later Sheriff Gibbs entered, followed by Chief Clark. Three uniformed attendants blocked the doorway.

"What's going on here?" demanded the Sheriff.

"An accessory after the fact in the killing of Mrs. Mona Thompson," stated Brady. "Clark, I want this man locked up and nobody permitted to see him. If you disobey my instructions you go to jail. All Thompson can do is fire you."

"If Gibbs repeats your instructions, Mr. Brady, I'll have to obey them," said Clark mournfully.

Gibbs cast a shrewd look at Brady.

"I'm telling yer, Chief," he said.

He saw them handcuff Mr. Hopkins and lead him toward the exit; then he rang for an attendant.

"Where did they put Miss Sterling?" he demanded.

"In rest room four, sir."

"Where is Diblee, the physical instructor?"

"In rest room two, sir."

"Anybody with the patients?"

"Mr. Overman is with Miss Sterling. Mrs. Jane Thompson and Dr. Olden are with Mr. Diblee."

"You mean that Mrs. Jane Thompson is with Diblee?" stammered the detective.

The man grinned. "Yes, sir. She's taking on something terrible."

Brady scratched his head and a slow grin spread over his face. Jane Thompson, Coleman's sweetie, was with Gomez and in distress.

Jane wasn't a two-timer. She was a three-timer. She had an intrigue with Coleman and a love affair with the physical instructor. And Coleman had got wise. Learning that both the giant and the detective were in the conduits, he had opened the valves which turned the water of the pond into the tunnel, had closed the watertight door. He had proposed to kill two birds with one stone.

Brady snapped his fingers. Why, he had a motive for the killing of Mona Thompson. Clinging to the notion that the murder was a female job, he had been unable to think of a powerful reason why any of the women at Thompson's house should wish to slay Thompson's wife.

Suppose that Jane, in love with Gomez, had discovered that the giant and his former wife had become lovers once more. She was a beautiful, passionate and unprincipled woman—a woman who wouldn't hesitate to kill her rival.

But there remained to be explained why Gomez, alias Diblee, was so filled with murderous hate against the detective that he had made numerous efforts against his life. If he had not killed Mona and was not one of Coleman's mob, and if he had resumed relations with his ex-wife, he should have been more eager than anybody else to have the murderer run down by the detective.

"Take me to room two," he commanded.

26

TURPITUDE OF JANE JEROME

"YOU'LL HAVE TO undress, sir."

"I'm in charge here, young man. Do as you're told."

"Yes, sir," said the man meekly. He cocked his head. "The private telephone is ringing," he said.

"What's that, a line to the Castle?"

"I don't know, sir. Mr. Hopkins always answered it himself."

Jack hesitated. There were two phones on the manager's desk.

"Which is it?" he inquired. The man pointed. No doubt King Tom had been informed of Hopkins's arrest. He would be raging and he might say something indiscreet. Brady picked up the instrument.

"Connect me with the police station, quick," said a very familiar voice.

"Bill Duffy!" cried the detective. Bill, whom he feared had been shot and thrown overboard by Coleman between the smugglers' hangout and the village of Santa Rosalita.

"Jack!" cried Duffy. "Where the devil are you? I came here looking for your body."

"Came where? Where are you?"

"At Saltelito. I found a telephone in a house here and I thought I could get the police."

"It's a private line to the office of the Nudist Club. Clear out of there immediately, Bill. There is a madman on his way."

"Oh, we like it here," said Bill with a chuckle. "Gertie and I think it would be a swell place for a honeymoon. How come you're at the Nudist Club?"

"I haven't time to go into that. You found her, did you? Well, scram out of there. You'll get your heads blown off."

"Oh, that's been tried," said Duffy with a mad laugh. "A bimbo had the nerve to show up in Gertie's speed boat while we were looking for a poor dumb detective. We hid in the house you went into and he came right in to call on us. I've got him trussed up like a Christmas turkey. That's why I want the cops to take him off our hands. Charge, swiping a motor boat from my fiancée and kidnaping and what not."

"Old man," said Brady excitedly, "can you hold the fort an hour? That's Coleman, the head of the smuggling gang, you have there."

"Gertie says his name is Rennick."

"Alias. I'll be there in an hour with the Sheriff. Watch him closely. He's about the most dangerous man alive."

"Well," said Bill, "he certainly doesn't look it. He barged in here and was he surprised when he looked into the muzzle of my revolver?"

"I thought you were unarmed."

Bill laughed loudly. "One picks up weapons in the strangest places. I'll be seeing you," he declared and hung up.

In high spirits, Brady placed the receiver on the hook. Coleman was caught—trussed up in the same house where he had captured the detective. No danger of his butting in while Jack did what had to be done here. Good old Duffy. If he ever lost his newspaper job Jack Brady had a good one for him in his New York agency.

"Let's go call on Mr. Diblee," he said to the attendant.

The men's locker room was full of members hastily dressing. The near tragedy had spoiled the day for the nudists, who were eager to get away. The attendant led Jack across the drawing room, through the dining room and down a corridor with doors on the left hand side. He opened the door of number two. A nude man and a nude woman were seated at the bedside of a huge form covered with a sheet.

They did not stir when Brady entered and closed the door behind him. Jack picked up a blanket from the foot of the bed and threw it over the shoulders of Jane Thompson, who started, turned and gazed up at him with tragic eyes.

"What's the verdict, doctor?" the detective asked softly.

Doctor Olden, who had a heavy brown mustache and a long solemn face, shook his head from side to side.

"Compound fracture. Very, very serious. He must be removed to the hospital. I can't understand what delays the ambulance."

"Will he recover?"

"It is very doubtful, sir."

Jack sighed. He hated to take life, even when it was necessary to save his own.

He laid his hand upon the shoulder of the beautiful young woman.

"Mrs. Thompson," he said, "I am forced to arrest you for the murder of your stepmother."

SHE LOOKED UP at him without the slightest change of expression.

"I don't care," she said. "He's going to die. But I'm sorry I killed Mona."

"Really!" exclaimed the doctor. "I protest! I never heard anything so ridiculous. She's wild with grief. She doesn't know what she is saying."

"Your patient is unconscious," said Brady firmly. "And this business won't wait. Mrs. Thompson has confessed to murder and you are a witness.

"Mrs. Thompson, you killed your stepmother because you caught this man making love to her, didn't you?"

The woman made a feeble gesture. "It was a misunderstanding. I didn't know he had been married to her."

"Tell why you did it, in your own way."

"I was in the Castle grounds one night and I saw him enter her room by the balcony. I thought, if she was out of the way, he would love me again. And the next afternoon I found her asleep on the Club roof. There was nobody near and she was so beautiful I went mad. I—I took a pillow and I smothered her with it. I am very strong."

"Mrs. Thompson!" gasped the horrified doctor.

"And it was all a mistake," she said in a low tone. "I wronged him terribly. You see I didn't know they had been married. She sent for him and implored him to take her away. She wanted Arthur to take her to the mainland that night. He refused. If I had only known then—"

"You confessed your crime to this man here?"

"Yes, and he forgave me. He is so wonderful. Doctor, don't let him die."

Brady now saw clearly.

"And when I arrived on the island he wanted to save you from the consequences of your crime and he tried to get rid of me, didn't he?"

"He loved me. He would do anything to save me. He hadn't loved Mona for years. Oh, if I had only known before it was too late."

Jack ruthlessly pursued his advantage. The woman was numb and indifferent at this moment; later she would be intensely aware of the awful consequences of her confession.

"If you love Arthur Gomez so much why, this morning, were you confiding in Rennick—Sam Coleman, if you know him by his real name?"

"I knew who he was. Coleman is in love with me. He confessed to me that he and my father-in-law were smuggling on a large scale. I was afraid Arthur might not be able to help me so I used Coleman. I told him that my father-in-law had killed his wife and that you had found evidence against him."

"I am horrified!" exclaimed the physician. "Such turpitude—"

"Be quiet," snapped Brady. "Mrs. Thompson, where did you get the revolver with which you chased a man you supposed to be me through the conduit?"

"Coleman keeps weapons in a locker in the inner storeroom where we were talking. We went in there because my husband and Arthur were both on the grounds and I didn't want them to know I was friendly with Coleman."

"How could you love Arthur and intrigue with this criminal at the same time?"

"I had no love for Coleman but I had to make use of him. I knew he was very crafty."

"Are you going to remember all this, doctor?" demanded Brady.

"It is indelibly engraved on my memory," said the physician gravely.

The woman's mood changed. She gazed defiantly at the detective.

"You never would have found out if this hadn't happened to my lover," she cried. "He's goin' to die and I don't care what happens to me."

"Come," said Brady sternly. "You must get dressed, you know."

She rose slowly.

"I know," she said. "Good-by, Arthur darling. I'll never see you again."

She bent and kissed him on the lips. He lay there without movement or consciousness.

AS SHE TURNED to go the door was pulled open and William Thompson, still nude, appeared.

"We're all leaving, Jane," he said testily. "Mr. Brady, you've violated the Club rules! What business have you here? I'll speak to my father about this."

Jack became suddenly conscious that he was dressed and he blushed.

"I'm sorry," he said. "Please accept my apologies."

"I'll meet you in the reception room, William," said Jane Thompson coolly. "Hurry and get your clothes on."

William turned grumpily away.

"Please don't tell my husband until I am dressed," she requested Brady.

He followed her to the entrance of the woman's locker room, passed through the men's room and stationed himself in the reception room into which the murderess had to emerge.

He had no sympathy for her, despite her beauty and the reality of her grief for the dying giant. She was a thoroughly self-centered person, without morals.

Because of her great beauty and charm it would be hard to get a jury to convict her. She would deny her confession, plead not guilty. Brady recognized that without her statement the case against her was circumstantial and full of holes. Her husband would stand by her like a gentleman.

Several minutes passed and then the door flew open and the maid rushed out of the women's room.

"Help!" she cried. "Mrs. Thompson is unconscious. I think she took poison."

Jack had a glimpse of several women inside, some of them nude, who were grouped about a form upon the floor.

"Take her to one of the rest rooms," Brady commanded, "and summon Dr. Olden from room two."

Most likely she had secured the poison after her crime, prepared to use it if it looked as though she would be accused of killing her mother-in-law. Well, she had saved the State the expense of a trial which would have resulted, probably, in an acquittal of a guilty woman.

The place was in confusion and Jack Brady still had work to do.

He left the Club, commandeered one of the three Thompson cars which were waiting without and drove to the pier. A few minutes later he was speeding toward Saltelito in a speed launch operated by an elderly boatman.

Things had come to a head. The murderer of Mona Thompson had confessed. The dope ring was smashed and King Tom of Santa Rosalita was powerless, now, to obstruct justice. Thanks to Bill Duffy, Coleman was waiting to be conducted to jail. In a situation like this the district attorney and sheriff of the county would have to do their duty.

27

TABLES TURNED

A FEW HOURS back, Brady had sat bound in a chair at Saltelito waiting for death. If Coleman's lust for vengeance hadn't persuaded the hophead to prolong the agony of his victim, Jane Thompson would be alive and going on with her love affair with the physical instructor. Gomez would be alive and well. Miss Sterling would not be suffering from an arrow wound and King Tom would be assured of the continuance of his revenue from dope, which enabled him to conceal the loss of his great fortune.

The innate decency of Oliver Thompson had been the weak point in the island system. If Ollie had shot down Bill Duffy when he attempted to escape in the outboard motor, Coleman would have murdered his prisoner in some peculiarly nasty way and all would have been well for the criminals.

Jack, who had some religion in his system, had a notion that Providence had taken a hand in the game played on Santa Rosalita Island.

As the boat approached the landing at Saltelito, he saw a black motor boat tied up there. Evidently Coleman, assuming he had escaped his captors, had not departed the way he came.

Jack leaped upon the pier just as the door of the cottage which had been his prison opened and a man in white linen came forth. Jack felt for his gun. He saw, almost immediately, that the man was a woman with golden hair.

"Who are you?" she called from afar.

"Name of Brady," he called back.

"We're waiting for you, Mr. Brady," she cried joyfully. She waited for him and he eyed her critically as he joined her.

"Suit of Coleman's best?" he inquired.

She laughed and nodded.

"Fits you pretty good. Got him tight in there?"

"Yes and Bill has his eye on him."

"Hum. You're a good looking gal. You going to marry that crazy reporter?"

"You should be crazy like he is," she said sharply. "Bill is a hero."

"Sure. All heroes are crazy. That's why they're heroes. He said you were his fiancée, over the phone."

"He took too much for granted."

Brady grinned and cast a sidelong glance at her.

"Oh, I don't know," he drawled. He pushed open the door of the cabin. Sam lay on the floor bound with the fishline which had held Jack Brady fast. His small eyes smoked at the sight of his enemy.

"About time you showed up," cried Bill Duffy. "What detained you?"

"Hello, Bill. Nice girl you have there. Sam, how's tricks?" He stood over the criminal, gazing down upon him with a mocking smile.

Sam drew back his upper lip and disdained to answer.

"So you let a couple of kids put it over on you," sneered Brady. "One of 'em a girl."

"How in hell did you get away from here?" asked Coleman, whose curiosity overcame his spleen.

"When I was a kid I worked for Houdini," replied Brady, who was in high good humor. "You should have stuck around at the Club, Sam. Big doings."

Sam didn't answer.

"Hopkins is in jail and Thompson can't get him out. We've found your cache of opium, Sam."

"Yeah?"

"Let's get going," said Brady breezily. "Cut him loose, Bill, while I put the bracelets on him. I'll lock him up in the island jail until it's time to take him to the mainland."

He saw Sam's eyes sparkle with hope and he laughed loudly.

"King Tom can't get you out, Sam," he said. "He's more apt to occupy the next cell. His reign is over, my boy, along with your racket."

He snapped the light steel handcuffs, which he always carried, upon the wrists of the dope runner, took his arm and pushed him out of doors. Bill and Gertrude followed them.

"I'll go in my boat with Sam," said Brady to his friends. "You kids follow in the black boat."

"How about the story?" demanded Duffy. "What's happened since I saw you last? Where's this cache of opium? How about the murderer of Mrs. Thompson?"

"As soon as I've seen the sheriff and locked up this crook," said Brady, "I'll meet you at the Rest House and spill everything. You know, Bill, I promised this yarn exclusive—"

"In view of the fact that I've done most of the work, including the capture of this crook who made a monkey out of you, I'm much obliged to you for your kindness," said Bill sardonically.

"You've been a help," Brady said. "But I've done a little research myself. Hop aboard the lugger, Sam."

HE FOUND CHIEF Clark almost on the verge of a nervous breakdown when he reached police headquarters.

"Thank God, you've come," he exclaimed. "Mr. Thompson has ordered me to release Mr. Hopkins."

"You're taking your orders from me, Clark. Lock this fellow up."

"But what has Mr. Rennick done?" demanded the chief.

"He's a dope smuggler. His real name is Coleman. Thompson will phone you to release him and I'm going to stay here to see that you don't."

Having seen Sam securely locked up, he seated himself in the office.

"Where's the sheriff?" he demanded.

"Up at the Castle. They're concluding the inquest."

"Phone him and the D.A. to hop down here. I'll tell them who killed Mrs. Thompson."

"That man in there?"

"You'd be surprised," retorted Brady with an exasperating smile.

Looking much perturbed, Chief Clark phoned Thompson's residence and demanded the sheriff.

"Mr. Brady is here with another prisoner," he said when

that official came on the line. "He asks you to suspend the inquest. He has the murderer."

"Had," corrected Brady sotto voce.

There was a wait of barely ten minutes and then a motor car was heard outside, the door was burst open and Thomas Thompson, in person, barged into the room, followed by the district attorney and the sheriff.

"Damn you, Brady," roared the island King, "What's all this, eh? How dare you make arrests without consulting me? How dare you force your way into the Nudist Club?"

"How are you, Mr. Thompson?" replied Brady suavely. "I've Snappy Sam Coleman locked up in there. I have a witnessed confession from the killer of Mrs. Thompson. I know exactly where the opium cache at the Nudist Club is located. I know who is Sam Coleman's partner in running millions of dollars worth of dope into the United States. This is Federal business, now, Mr. Thompson. Anything to say?"

Thompson's florid cheeks turned an ash color. His eyes glazed. He clenched his hands and for a moment he was speechless.

"You heard what I said, Mr. Crane," said Jack sternly. "Are you going to permit this man to obstruct justice?"

Crane glanced at the sheriff.

"I trail with Brady," said that officer.

"If you can substantiate your charges," said the district attorney, "I will do my damnedest to punish the offenders." He glanced at Thompson, whose alarm was obvious.

"I have no intention of obstructing justice," said the owner of the island. "I hear assertions from you, not proof. Who murdered my wife? That's what I want to know."

"Your daughter-in-law, Mrs. Jane Jerome Thompson," replied Brady.

THOMPSON LIFTED HIS big fist.

"She is dead," he shouted. "How dare you bring such a charge against the dead?"

"She took poison, as you no doubt know. She killed herself after I had confronted her with the evidence and after she had made a full confession in the presence of Dr. Olden."

"If that is so," Thompson said dully, "you have accomplished the work you were brought here to do. I'll pay your fee and you can go."

Brady shook his head. "A band of criminals have made their headquarters on this island, and used the Nudist Club as their headquarters. I hope to prove that they operated with your knowledge and connivance."

"I deny that. I deny every word of it," blustered Thompson.

"You'll have your chance in court. I won't put you under arrest, as you are too prominent an individual to make an attempt to escape. Sheriff, if you will come with me, I'll show you a cache of opium in an underground chamber at the Nudist Club. We are going with or without your permission, Mr. Thompson."

"It's a private club. Mr. Crane, I protest—"

"My dear Mr. Thompson," said the district attorney unctuously, "this is probably a mare's nest. But, since a detective of Mr. Brady's reputation makes the charge, an investigation is unavoidable."

Thompson turned and without a word strode out of the

station. The slump of his shoulders was significant to the men he left behind him.

"Chief Clark," said Brady, "In view of the fact that Thompson pays your salary, the escape of the two prisoners will cause you to be placed under arrest. As they are charged with a Federal offense, you'll get short shrift in a Federal court."

"I am taking orders from the sheriff of the county, Mr. Brady," retorted the chief. "No prisoner has ever escaped from this jail."

Jack didn't bother to make the obvious retort that the jail never before had held an important one.

"Come on, Gibbs," he said.

"It looks to me," remarked Gibbs as they hastened toward the Nudist Club, "as if Thompson was in on this. He certainly acted guilty."

"He's in on it," replied Brady "but it's going to be hard to prove it. Are the telephone lines to the mainland open again?"

"Yes. The break was repaired a few hours ago."

"We'll want to communicate at once with the Federal people. We'd better pick up the U. S. Customs man to make this search regular."

28

CONCLUSION

BRADY FOUND HIS newspaper friend waiting for him at the Guest House when he arrived there with the light of achievement in his eye.

"Gosh, I'm hungry," exclaimed the detective. "You can phone your story to the mainland, Bill. The cable has been repaired, if it was ever out of repair."

"I'm not hungry," replied Duffy. "Gertrude and I had a snack." He produced a wad of yellow paper and a pencil. "I'm taking this yarn to the mainland personally. Get started, will you? First the big stuff and then a narrative account of how you got it."

"I think you had better say 'we,'" Brady suggested. "You went blundering round and hit the right track before I did. By the way, I've some good news for you—"

"Come on. Who killed Mona Thompson and how and why? What did Coleman have to do with it—"

"O.K."

Duffy's eyes glittered feverishly and his pencil flew over the copy paper. For half an hour the detective talked with hardly an interruption. Brady had a gift for clear thinking and clear expression. All Bill had to do was take dictation and he had a splendid newspaper running story. Occasionally he grunted excitedly and sucked in his breath and scratched out words he had written so fast as to be illegible.

"What a yarn!" he cried when the detective reached his climax. "Boy, it has every element of drama and all the colors of the rainbow. And a clean beat—"

"Looks like your job was safe," remarked Brady.

"The heck with that. I'll get offers from the biggest papers in the country. Imagine using the Nudist Club as a blind for the dope business. Wow! It's sort of libelous, though, tying King Tom up to it. Think you can put it over? The yarn is so big I don't want it marred by a libel suit."

"I'm afraid I can't, Bill. Hopkins doesn't know who was his principal, in my opinion. Coleman will take his medicine without squealing. I could run down Oliver Thompson and make him testify but I'm not going to. I owe my life to the poor kid."

"But the circumstances are incriminating. The fact that he went broke a couple of years ago and continued to spend at the old rate. Where did he get his money? And the way the Nudist Club was honeycombed with underground passages. He must have told the architect to do that."

"I've inquired. Ten years ago there was a cloudburst on this island. The drains were alleged to be necessary in case of another one. It's a poor excuse, of course."

"What a story the trial of Jane Jerome Thompson would have made," said Bill regretfully. "Well, we can't have everything. What was the value of the opium you found hidden under the Nudist Club?"

"Nearly half a million dollars worth," said Brady.

"What becomes of it?"

"The government takes it. And here is the good news.

The government pays twenty-five per cent of its value to the person who brings about the seizure of smuggled goods. A hundred twenty-five thousand dollars. We split it."

"Eh?"

Brady grinned. "You discovered the conduit system. You checked the suspicion I had regarding smuggling. You captured the head of the dope ring, Sam Coleman. Now don't argue."

"Well," said Bill Duffy with a deep, rapturous sigh, "I won't." He rose. "I'll be seeing you, Jack."

"Going to rush right over to the mainland?"

"I'm going to phone them to hold open the two first pages. I'll go over a little later."

"Then what's your hurry?"

"I'm going up to see Gertie Smith."

"Oh, yes. Say, Bill, she's a nudist, isn't she?"

"If you're so dumb you can't see the difference between a brazen nudist and a working girl who massages women in a private room in the clubhouse—"

"But just the same she went round nude—"

"You," declared Bill Duffy furiously," can go to hell."

Leaving Jack Brady laughing heartily, the newspaperman rushed out of the hotel.

AS BRADY HAD anticipated, it was impossible for the government to convict King Tom of complicity in the smuggling conspiracy which had unloaded several millions of dollars worth of Chinese opium on American soil in about eighteen months. Snappy Sam went to a Federal prison for twenty years without opening his mouth.

Hopkins was a worthless witness and county officials were silent for fear of incriminating themselves.

Thompson's skillful lawyer eventually secured an acquittal, but the trial cost the former captain of industry what cash he still possessed. A blight struck Santa Rosalita Island.

Thompson, wounded in his most vital spot, his vanity, remains in his castle, gazing moodily down upon a dying resort. His parasites have fled. His steamship company is in a receiver's hands; so is his hotel. He lives on what income he receives from the sale of leased land to cottagers. Many of the permanent residents have moved away; the tourists go elsewhere.

Naturally, the order for his biography was cancelled; Owen Overman departed within a day or two after the funerals of Mona and Jane Thompson. He took Lida Sterling with him.

Bill Duffy scooped the country and received many flattering offers, but the publisher of the *Sphere* held him by giving him a block of stock in the newspaper. And he and Gertrude Smith were married a month after the bombshell of Santa Rosalita burst. Lieutenant-Commander and Mrs. Long, the former fiancée of Bill Duffy, were among the guests. When the slow moving government pays him his share of the reward, Bill expects to buy a half interest in the *Sphere*.

As for Jack Brady, he returned to New York with enhanced reputation. But he had to stand for a lot of joshing from his friends there for going nudist, even to serve the ends of justice.

www.ingramcontent.com/pod-product-compliance
Lightning Source LLC
Chambersburg PA
CBHW030544030726
47495CB00004B/1129